FLICKER

Flicker vertigo (also known as the Bucha effect)

An imbalance in brain-cell activity caused by exposure to low-frequency flickering (or flashing) of a relatively bright light. It is a disorientation-, vertigo-, and nausea-inducing effect of a strobe light flashing at 1 Hz to 20 Hz—approximately the frequency of human brainwaves.

The effects are similar to seizures caused by epilepsy, but are not restricted to people with histories of epilepsy.

Clarence E Rash: Awareness of Causes and Symptoms of Flicker Vertigo Can Limit Ill Effects: Human Factors and Aviation Medicine: Vol 51: Number 2: Mar-Apr 2004: Flight Safety Foundation.

FLICKER

Melanie Hooyenga

Left-Handed Mitten
Publications

FLICKER

Published by Left-Handed Mitten Publications

ISBN 1480200840
eBook ISBN 978-1480200845

UPC

Book design by the Ink Slinger Designs
Cover design by Ink Slinger Designs
Ebook formatting by The eBook Artisans

Author website: www.melaniehoo.com
Email: melaniehooyenga@gmail.com
Facebook: facebook.com/MelanieHooyenga

For gramma,
my fellow flickerer

Prologue

Sunlight pulses across the dashboard—light, dark, light, dark—and catches the dust dancing on the imitation leather.

My eyes stutter, but I blink it away. My heart jumps around in my chest. I stroke the grainy piece of cement stuck between my back teeth with my tongue. The orthodontist swore he got it all, but that was as true as his promise that it wouldn't be uncomfortable.

Uncomfortable. Right.

A tingling sensation pricks the tips of my fingers. I press them together, watching the blood shift beneath my skin. The tingling turns to those sharp needles that remind me of anything but sleep.

I press harder and my toes start tingling too. What the hell?

The dancing on the dashboard gets faster. The trees here are taller, straighter, and the sunlight strobes through the branches. My breath catches and a sudden heaviness pushes me deep into the seat.

I glance at Mom but she's concentrating on the road, humming along with golden oldies or whatever the hell it is she listens to, oblivious to the fact that something very weird is happening to her daughter.

To me.

I close my eyes. The heaviness lifts. Too much. Now I'm floating and—

"But Mom, I'm fine."

Mom crosses the kitchen and leans against the counter. "Biz, you're going. The dentist said your face will change if you don't get braces. Your entire face could look different…"

A sense of déjà vu slams me over the head. I've had this argument. Next Mom is gonna grab the stack of mail that Dad left on the counter and toss it in the basket.

She does.

"Biz?"

The words tumble out of me. "Mom…" The déjà vu doesn't lift. This isn't a memory. I'm not in the car anymore.

I've gone back to yesterday.

Chapter 1

I've been flickering—jumping back to yesterday—since I was thirteen. The first time I thought the orthodontist gave me more laughing gas than he was supposed to, but in the four years since then I figured out I can use the light to my advantage. I've retaken tests, undone fights with friends, and repeated more than a few memorable dates.

Unfortunately this is not one of those times.

Music blares from a speaker in the corner of the gymnasium, the heavy bass vibrating through me and everyone else flailing on the dance floor. A disco ball throws flashes of light spiraling off every surface in the room. I throw my head back and close my eyes, pretending to lose myself in the music, when really I'm just trying to block out the damn light.

"I love this song!" Amelia, my best friend, grabs my arm and bounces next to me. Her dark wavy hair sways with the music, unlike mine which hangs limp over my shoulders.

My eyes open a slit. "Didn't disco balls go out in the 70s?"

She laughs, a throaty giggle that makes me smile. "So keep your eyes closed. I won't let you run into anyone."

Yeah, right. I sway next to Amelia, scanning the crowd for Robbie, my boyfriend, and spot him against the far wall laughing with a couple friends. His blond hair practically glows in the blinking lights. He notices me watching him and smiles. As I lift my hand to give a half-hearted wave a low chuckle behind me makes me turn.

"How long did you promise to dance?" Cameron, my other best friend, stands flat-footed with his arms crossed, indifferent to the movement surrounding us. His dark eyes twinkle, a smile lifting the corner of his mouth.

Amelia spins, sending her hair flying. "Three songs! This is number two."

"And thank god it's almost over."

She laughs. "Come on, Biz, you love it." She throws an arm over my shoulder and we knock hips.

Cam nods at our friends near Robbie. "I'll be over there."

The song ends and the blinking lights slow to a lazy loop around the room. Crap. I also promised Robbie one slow dance, and from the look on his face as he weaves through the couples already pressed close together, I'm not getting out of this.

He smiles. "They're playing our song."

"We don't have a song"

"I know, but I requested it so that makes it our song." His lips graze my cheek and he places my hands behind his neck. Our bodies brush as we turn in a small circle. "Is this really so bad?" he whispers.

"No." I rest my head against his shoulder. My eyes close but my thoughts are anything but relaxed. This is supposed to be what I want. A boy who wants to dance with me and spend time with me and seems to think I'm cute. So why do I feel so antsy when he's around? I mean, I know why—he's hardly the first boy I've dated and I always get this feeling after a couple months. But why can't I just be happy?

Robbie trails his fingers up and down my back, then pushes

my hair off my shoulder. His warm breath on my neck gives me the shivers, but it's not the reaction he was going for.

I pull away. "I think I need to get some air."

He looks at me tenderly, misinterpreting my signals. "Okay."

I turn away and push through our classmates, but he grabs my hand, stopping me. I face him.

His eyes are clearer, the smile gone. "You don't have to run away from me. I'll come with you."

Whatever. I let him lead me into the hallway, but he turns around a corner into a darker corridor. "Robbie, wait." I stop, his fingers still linked through mine. This isn't what I want.

"Biz, you just said you wanted to get some air." He does air quotes around the last part.

"It wasn't code for making out. I really needed to get out of there. The lights..." My fingers touch the side of my head. That's the downside of flickering. I get wicked migraines that sometimes last longer than the time I flickered. But it's usually worth it, and I've gotten used to the constant headaches.

He rolls his eyes. "It's practically pitch black in there."

I've never explained my deal with light to Robbie, and I sure as hell am not going to clue him in now. "Forget it."

His hand snakes around my neck and he tries to pull me close.

My hands flatten against his chest. "Robbie…" I warn.

A noise behind us makes me turn. Cam is standing at the end of the corridor, bathed in light from the main hallway. And he's glaring at Robbie.

Robbie looks at Cam then scowls back at me. "If I didn't know better I'd think he's your boyfriend." He releases my neck and stalks down the dark hall, away from me and Cam.

"You know that's not true," I say to his back.

"What do you see in him anyway?" Cameron's at my side, his hands stuffed in his jeans pockets. His hair falls over his eyes as he looks down at me.

"I don't know anymore."

He smiles. "Well you still owe Amelia one more dance, then everyone's heading to the boat ramp for the after-party."

I sigh dramatically. "Fine. As long as you promise to help me drag her out of there. She's eyeballing the soccer team and if I know her she won't want to leave until she talks to one of them."

"Deal."

I glance over my shoulder to see if Robbie's still there, but he's gone. I should probably feel guilty or worried or something, but all I feel is relief.

◆ ◆ ◆

On Monday Robbie stops me in the hall after trig class. "How'd you do on the quiz?"

I guess he's not mad at me anymore. "Not well. Why'd Bishop make you stay?"

"Just giving me crap because I didn't finish." He slips his arm around me and tugs me down the hall.

I don't mean to stiffen, but my body pauses. I avoided his calls all weekend but I guess he didn't get the hint.

"What?" Frustration laces his words and the corners of his eyes crinkle the way they do when he's about to go off on someone.

"Nothing. I just…" Don't like the fact that you've gotten too close to me. "I didn't finish the quiz either and I'm worried I'm gonna fail."

Robbie follows me to my locker and waits while I switch my

books. "That's not it. You've been acting weird since before the dance." He touches my arm, a gesture that used to send ripples through me but now makes me want to scratch where he touched, as if that would undo his caress.

I turn to look at him. "It's nothing. I'm just worried about my dad." I hate myself for playing the sympathy card, but it's the easiest way to deflect attention from what's really bothering me.

He drops his hand and his eyes soften. "Did something happen?"

I close my locker. Nothing happened, but that doesn't mean I don't live in an eternal state of worrying about my dad, something most of the kids in school would never understand. "No, but thanks for asking." I hurry down the hall before he can press further, his eyes burning into my back. I feel like a complete bitch for not telling him the truth.

Chapter 2

Sunlight filters through the low hanging clouds as I drive along the river. Thank god there won't be any flickering today. I'm worried about how bad I did on the quiz, but I don't think it really makes a difference at this point. Bishop knows I don't give a shit about math and as long as I pass the rest of my classes I should be fine. Or at least that's what I keep telling myself.

The shades in my house are drawn when I park in my spot next to the giant pine tree.

This can't be good.

I race through the front door, scanning the couch, the kitchen, the bathroom, trying to find Dad. I find him in bed, reading.

Dropping the book to his chest, his smile loosens the tension in my shoulders.

"I thought you had another—"

"I wish you'd stop worrying about me so much. I'm tired so I decided to read until you got home. Now that you are, I'll get up." Tossing the covers aside, he swings his pajama-ed legs over the side of the bed. "Did the school tell you about the kidnapping?"

"Kidnapping?" I mentally skip through to the jumble of texts I received today, but I would have remembered something like that.

Pain creases his face as he stands. "Little girl. I think they said she was seven."

"Is seven."

He cocks his head at me.

"You don't know that she's dead. I hate when people talk like someone is dead when you don't know." Crossing my arms over my chest, I'm not sure why I picked this as my battle today. Dad certainly doesn't deserve this.

"Sorry. She is seven. I guess she stayed home from school because she was sick, but her mom let her play in the yard after lunch."

"Someone just took her?" My thoughts jump to Cameron, the only person I know who had someone taken like that. Katie's disappearance devastated his family and changed Cam from a carefree kid to someone more serious, more cautious.

"I know I don't have to tell you this, but I'm going to. Be careful," he says, taking a step closer and resting a shaky hand on my arm.

"I will," I say, sliding my hand over his, still thinking of Cameron. They never found out what happened to his sister. No body, nothing.

"Are you okay?" The cloudiness that sometimes masks his eyes has lifted and his clear blue eyes bore into mine. He squeezes my fingers and for a second, they tingle.

That's weird. Usually I only feel that when—

"Biz?"

Oh right. "Yeah, I'm fine. This made me think of Cameron's sister. I hope this girl's family doesn't have to go through what they did." Endless searches, her hand linked together with Cameron's as they picked their way through the forest with a hundred other people, Cameron's mom sobbing in their pickup truck. They found a sock that could have been hers, but nothing more.

Then the accusations. Cam getting dragged out of school by the police, everyone whispering that since he was the last one to see Katie alive he must know more than he was saying.

Dad steers me into the hallway and down the stairs. "Do you need help with your homework?"

A sigh escapes me before I can stop it. "Probably. Trig is kicking my ass." I flinch when he swats my arm. "Sorry, but it is!"

"I know you don't like math, and yes, you won't need it once you're done with school, but you need to graduate before you can be done with it," He says, sinking into his spot on the couch. I curl up on the opposite end. "What about your other classes? I'd rather know before I get a note that you're failing."

I feel guilty for a minute, but I push it aside. I try, I really do, but certain things just don't stick in my head. I figure that something needs to be forgotten to make up for whatever space the flickering takes up. "No failing grades." Yet, I add silently. "We get our next photojournalism assignment tomorrow."

"Well I'm glad you have at least one class to look forward to." A reflection from outside flashes light through the living room. Instinctively I turn away, just as my dad closes his eyes. His voice comes out much softer than before. "You're talented, Biz. Don't be afraid to go after something you really want."

◆ ◆ ◆

I grab my camera and go outside, Mr. Turner's lecture on f-stops droning in my head. Not that f-stops don't interest me—they're crucial if you actually plan to be a photographer, which I do—but I already know everything he covered. I signed up for Intro to Photojournalism to learn more about telling a story with my photos.

Crouching low to the ground, I prop my elbows on my knees, my camera balanced in my hands. I check the settings, then press the button. Click-click-click. Turner helped me program the camera to take three pictures with one push. Said it's a trick the pros use because it allows you to fully capture the moment. Or something like that. It's supposed to work great for action shots, but it's a bit of overkill for Mom's flower bed.

I flick a switch and scrutinize the shots. Yep, flowers. Each shot nearly identical.

With a heavy sigh I fall backwards until I'm stretched on the grass, the camera resting on my chest. The setting sun casts shadows over the side of the house, washing away the color my father painstakingly painted last summer. By taking away the light, the pigment disappears too.

I jerk upright and the camera is at my face before I'm even thinking. Click-click-click. But I don't stop there. I don't know what exactly I'm hoping to accomplish, but I can't resist whatever's drawing me to the shadows.

"Biz?" Mom calls from the doorway. "Can you get dinner out of the oven and set the table? I'm helping your dad."

"Sure thing." Brushing grass from my jeans, I pick up my camera and head to the kitchen, where the mouthwatering aroma of three-cheese lasagna nearly knocks me over. "This makes up for my day." Hot pads in hand, I pull the casserole dish from the oven and slide it onto the table. Next, plates and silverware, then I reach into the cupboard above the phone and grab the basket of pills.

I could count them out with my eyes closed, the distinct shape and size of each pill more familiar than the multi-vitamin Mom made me start taking last year, but I'm a good daughter and I check each bottle, careful to only take from the bottles marked "Twice a day." I drop the pills into the ceramic dish on the table, the white tablets stark against the reds, oranges, and purples baked into the piece of pottery.

My finger traces the yellow swirl that loops around the rim. Ironic that the two dollar souvenir from my parents' honeymoon—a trip that also resulted in me—has become such an integral part of our lives. Mom says that when she picked it out in that dusty artisan market she figured it'd get tossed into a drawer and never be seen again. Yet here it is, in the place of honor—

"Hey, sweetie. Get anything good?"

I whirl around.

Dad stands in the doorway, his face twisted between a grimace and a smile. He's fighting it, but the grimace is winning. His black hair is freshly combed, the part straighter than the rest of him would ever be.

I know that look. "Another one?"

He shrugs.

"I knew I shouldn't have left so early this morning." I forgot to set out his meds before leaving for school.

"Biz, it's not your fault."

"Did you take your pills?"

His eyes dart to the table, brush over the Mexico bowl. "Yeah." He doesn't meet my gaze.

"Dad, you have to take them. This happens every time you forget—"

"I've already heard it from your mother."

"Well—"

Mom joins him in the doorway and runs the back of her fingers across his cheek. "He promised to be better about taking them." She smiles. "Although I think he would have promised anything to keep me from calling the ambulance."

My head snaps between them. "It was that bad?"

Dad still refuses to look at me.

Mom crosses the kitchen, stopping in front of the table and the little ceramic bowl. Our ironic icon. She scoops up the pills, walks back to Dad, and slips them into his hand. "Yeah, it was."

Chapter 3

A piercing whistle quiets the auditorium.

Principal Walker, better known as Stride Right, shuffles to the center of the stage. Rumor has it he has some kind of issue with his name and refuses to walk like a normal person. The nickname's been around since way before I got to high school.

Stride Right clears his throat. "As most of you have heard by now, a seven-year old girl was kidnapped yesterday. Most of you are probably wondering what this has to do with you." He turns on his heel and half marches to one side of the stage, peering into the darkness behind the curtain. He lifts a hand and waves for someone to approach. "Officer Jackson is here to talk to you about safety."

A heavyset man with thinning hair and bad skin steps into the spotlight. His blue uniform strains against his belly, his gun rests comfortably at his side.

I turn away as a murmur rises up from the students.

Stride Right goes on. "I know. You know everything there is about being safe. Humor me," he says before shuffling into the darkness of the wings, leaving the cop staring at us, arms stiff at his sides.

"Common sense will save you in most situations. Unfortunately," he chuckles, "not a lot of you have any common sense, so that's why I'm here."

This is the person our fine police station chose to send to our school? As he drones on, I twist around in my seat to find Amelia. We had to sit with our class and she's towards the back of the room. A sharp cough draws my eye near the aisle and Amelia's dark head pops up.

"Did you have a question, miss?"

Her head disappears.

"Kids, this is a serious matter. I know you think you've got better things to worry about, but your safety is the priority of this school, the police department, and your families."

My eyes skim the faces, hoping to find someone as bored as I am, and land on Cameron. He isn't smiling. Several kids turn to look at him, then stare across the auditorium at me. Heat flushes my cheeks and I sink lower in my seat.

Safety. Right. I can at least pretend to pay attention to the rest of the speech.

◆ ◆ ◆

Robbie's waiting for me at my locker. "I texted you last night..."

A lie springs to my lips but the hurt in his eyes stops me. "I'm sorry, I—"

"I don't get it. You always have your phone on you."

That's true. I got each of his texts the instant they came through. I just couldn't make myself reply.

He stares at the ground, the confidence I'd once found so endearing gone.

Guilt pummels me, but there's no sense in dragging this out. "Robbie, this isn't working for me anymore. You're a great guy and all but—"

He looks up. "You're serious? Just like that?" He shakes his head and his gaze drops to the floor. "But what about…?" he trails off.

I bite my lip.

He leans close and his dark eyes turn cold. "I should've listened when everyone told me to stay the hell away from you. What a waste of time."

My reputation may have a benefit after all. I watch him go, unable to move until the bell sounds. Late for class, I slam my locker shut and hurry to photojournalism.

At least I won't fail in there.

◆ ◆ ◆

"Biz, these are remarkable." Turner clicks through my photos a third time. "You have a remarkable eye for detail, especially considering this is your first photography class."

My head drops forward until my hair covers my face. Until this year I hadn't taken photography seriously and while I love hearing that I'm doing well, I'm not used to getting compliments.

"Don't be embarrassed. It took me until I was in my thirties to discover my passion. You have a gift and you should be proud of it."

"Mm-hmm." I want to hear this, I really do, but couldn't he just text me or something? Hearing people say nice things out loud is just weird. Especially a teacher.

He clears his throat and waits until I meet his eye. "The assignment was flora so you can't use these—" he holds up a hand when my mouth drops open, "—for class. But I'd like you to submit them to the paper."

"Oh, sure." No one actually reads the Weekly Digest. It's a glorified gossip rag for the kids in the newspaper club. And not even good gossip.

He continues clicking through my photos.

"So do I just talk to the club advisor?"

His eyes narrow and his head tilts slightly to the side. "What? Why—oh! I don't mean the school paper." He chuckles and my cheeks burn. "I meant the Daily Chronicle."

Now it's my turn to be confused. "But why would they want my pictures?"

"Biz, I'm trying to tell you that you have talent. Something that will stay with you long after you've finished high school." He sets the camera on his desk. "Getting published in a real publication is just the first step."

"You really think these are good enough? They're just of the side of my house."

"A friend of mine runs the features section and he's always looking these types of photos. I'll give you his email and you can submit them that way."

I bristle despite myself. "I don't need any favors."

He exhales heavily. "I appreciate that you think I have that much control over what is published in our local paper, but believe me, I don't. All I'm giving you is the connection. The rest is up to you."

I head back to my desk, allowing a small smile to creep over my face, but it vanishes when I look up and see Cameron watching me. Seeing his clenched jaw and narrowed eyes reminds me of my conversation with Robbie and I'm filled with a heavy feeling of guilt.

◆ ◆ ◆

Driving home after school I can't help but replay what Robbie said. I know people started saying shit about me after I dumped Alex a couple months ago, but it's not because I don't like them. It's totally the opposite. If they get too close…

My fingers tingle. I flex them against the steering wheel, but it's too late to stop it. The rhythmic pulse of light floods through the drivers' side window. My reflex is to close my eyes but I can't keep them shut.

The tingling moves up my hands, delicate pinpricks that increase in intensity until the sensation races up my arms and slams into my chest. The familiar heaviness pushes me against the seat and I fight the urge to stare into the light. The test wasn't that bad. I can deal with failing. It's reliving that conversation with Robbie that I'd rather avoid.

I reach for my sunglasses in the passenger seat but it's too late.

With a final push the heaviness lifts and I'm floating, barely able to hang on to the steering wheel. I take a deep breath and—

—I'm in yesterday's English class. A couple people look at me from the corner of their eye but no one says anything.

When I come to after flickering, I spasm like when you dream that you're falling. Sometimes I do it on purpose when I'm not flickering. I figure the more people think I'm just mildly weird, the less likely they are to know how weird I really am.

Chapter 4

One of the down sides of flickering is reliving things I'd rather not repeat. Like the safety assembly with Stride Right. It was bad enough the first time, having to watch him strut around like he's all important, but listening to him a second time is unbearable.

I focus on a piece of hair dangling from the collar of the girl in front of me. It flutters in a breeze I can't feel, then drifts to the darkness at my feet.

While I'm staring at the floor a sense of dread sneaks up on me. I lean my head back on the seat and close my eyes. How can I do it better this time?

"Common sense will save you in most situations. Unfortunately," the cop chuckles, "not a lot of you have any common sense, so that's why I'm here."

Oh good, it's almost over.

The same hushed whispers pass through the auditorium after the cop leaves the stage. I want nothing more than to sneak out the back door, but I spot Cameron ahead of me, walking alone, the other kids moving around him like they're afraid to get too close. If he can face the entire school and the things they say about him, I can deal with one boy.

Robbie's at my locker. "I texted you last night..."

This time I stop the lie before it can form, but the hurt is still in his eyes. "Robbie, I think we need to talk."

His eyes dart to my locker, then down at our feet.

Words won't come.

He looks up. "You don't want to see me anymore?"

Huh? My brows crinkle and my heart drops to my stomach. How did he know that?

"You've been acting different the past couple weeks. That's why I wanted to talk to you last night."

"It is?" Don't tell me he wanted to break up with me.

He toes the ground with his sneaker and leans against the locker. "There's no point dragging this out if you aren't feeling it. Besides, I knew what people said about you before we started going out."

I really can't escape my reputation.

"You're a great guy and all but—"

"Don't go there." He leans close but his dark eyes don't have the same coldness they did last time. "I just wish you'd had the balls to say something when you decided we were over."

"What do you mean?" I mean, I know what he means, but how could he know that's how I felt?

"You walk around like you've got some secret you don't want to share. I thought that maybe when we started dating you'd let me in, but I don't know you any better than I did two months ago." He gives the locker a final shove before turning on his heel and stalking away.

I don't feel the same anguish as before, but this still sucks. I close my locker and walk slowly to class.

◆ ◆ ◆

This time I grab a hat from my locker and shove on my sunglasses before venturing home. I've learned that no matter how many things I'm able to change, the weather isn't one of them. If it's sunny today, it's sunny today.

Feeling the warmth wash over me, I grip the steering wheel and take slow, deep breaths. After a few hard blinks, my eyes finally focus. That's something else I've figured out. I can't be jumping back every time I'm in a car or train, as I realized too late on my freshman field trip, so I'm teaching my body to fight what comes naturally.

Up ahead is a section of road I call the Strand. There's nothing special about this particular chunk of black top, at least not to anyone else. For me it's where I come when I want to flicker. The precision of the farmer who planted these trees dozens of year ago, combined with the angle of the mid-afternoon sun, makes it my go-to place when I need to go back.

I usually take different routes home on the days I want to... well, continue with my day, but Robbie has me distracted.

His words hit me harder than I thought they would. Maybe because I expected him to change what he said. But flickering doesn't change who I am, or why I can't let anyone get too close.

It's not fair to him, or anyone else that really tries to get to know me, but I can't risk anyone knowing the truth. If I let them get too close I might slip up, and who knows what might happen to me. I've seen what they do to my dad—the needles, the brain scans, more drugs than anyone should have to take without getting some kind of pleasure out of it—and he has a legitimate disease. I don't need some doctor poking around inside my skull to tell me something I already know.

I'm a freak.

Chapter 5

I breathe a sigh of relief when I pull into the driveway. So many people take it for granted that when you get in your car and drive someplace you'll actually get there. I'm especially happy to be home. It's not much, but it's a haven for me, even though my parents don't know about my condition. Since they don't have any other kids to compare me to they probably assume my quirks are just normal teenage stuff.

Dad's on the couch reading with the TV on low. Neither one of us can stand complete silence. My solution is my iPod, but I haven't been able to convince him to get one for himself. He says he's happy with the boob tube.

Dropping my bag against the coffee table, I sink into the spot next to him.

His eyebrow lifts, his clear eyes studying me. "Rough day?"

"You could say that." I feel like I haven't slept in two days. Because I haven't.

"Anything you need to talk about?"

Let's see. I dumped my boyfriend—twice—and the guys at school apparently have some sort of warning system about me. "Not really. A cop came to school to talk to us about safety. Because of that kidnapping." My fingers drift to my temple before I catch myself.

His frown deepens. "Another one?"

"Not yet. But soon."

"Mom refilled your prescription last week. There should be a new bottle in your bathroom."

My parents know I get migraines, they just don't know why. No one does. So far I've been able to skate through doctors' appointments without any kind of brain scans. God knows what the hell they'd find inside my head.

Dad pats my leg and smiles. "Go take something and lie down for a little while. I'll wake you up for dinner."

I nod at the kitchen and the ceramic bowl I know is on the table. "Did you take yours?"

His smile tightens. "Of course."

◆ ◆ ◆

Music plays just loud enough to drown out the silence. Any louder and Dad will pester me about needing to rest. I grab my cell phone from the front pocket of my bag and press Amelia's name.

"Dude, what's up? I saw you talking to Robbie in the hall and he did not look happy." Amelia never was one to beat around the bush.

I sigh.

"Really? I thought you liked him."

And this is why Amelia is my best friend. Most times I don't even have to tell her what's going on and she knows. That makes it hard with the stuff I have to keep from her, but I love not having to explain my every waking thought about everything else.

"I do. I mean, I did. I just..." I'm gonna have to come up with a better explanation than this. You'd think I'd be used to it by now. "I guess it got boring."

Amelia laughs. "You mean now that you got him it's boring. One of these days you're gonna to have to stick around once the chasing part is over."

My fingers curl tightly around the phone. "Is that what people say about me? That I just play games? Because that's totally not what I'm about."

Her laughter stops. "Sorry. No, that's not what I mean. It's just," she clears her throat, "you've never dated anyone more than a couple months. I know we're not trying to get married or anything, but you've got a track record, babe."

I flop back on my bed and stare at the ceiling. "You have a point." It's not the right point, but it's a point.

The music on her end gets louder and she raises her voice to compensate. "So what'd you think of Stride Right's little talk today?"

"Ugh, don't remind me. I felt like it went on forever."

"And that cop! What an ass." Amelia inhales sharply. "Did you see Cameron in there?"

Cameron's dark features sweep through my mind and I remember the way he stopped me in my tracks two different times today. Well, really four, but who's counting? "Yeah, and I'm worried about him."

"Because of his sister?"

"Well yeah. This hasn't happened since Katie disappeared."

"Do you think the police will want to talk to him again?"

I'd thought of nothing else since I last saw him. Normally I'd have talked to him by now but it occurs to me that I haven't actually spoken to him since class yesterday.

A light knock on my door interrupts my thoughts.

"Hey, I gotta go. I'm supposed to be sleeping and someone's at my door."

"Another migraine?"

"One's on its way."

"Will you be in school tomorrow?"

"Yeah." If I skipped every time I had a headache I'd be twenty-four before I graduated. I toss the phone across the floor and roll so I'm facing the wall. "Come in."

"Is it bad?"

I shift to my back as Mom sits on the edge of the bed. As if on cue a sharp stab pierces through my right ear towards the top of my head. "Not yet."

She touches the side of my face, her cool fingers winding their way through my hair until they're tucked behind my ear and pressing into the base of my skull, just the way I like it. "I worry about you. It seems like they're coming more often."

Only when I fail tests. Or forget to pay attention to where I'm at.

"Your dad and I want bring you in for more tests."

But he's on my side! I sit up and her hand drops to my shoulder. "Really? Dad said that?"

She lowers her hand to her lap and twists her wedding band. "Well, it was my idea and he didn't disagree. At least not much."

That makes me feel a little better.

"I hate seeing you like this. You've lost weight and sometime your eyes seem… I don't know… hollow. Like there's something eating away at you."

My hand moves over hers. I lean close to look in her eyes. "Mom, I'm fine. The pills work great and I just need to try to get more sleep. Please don't make me go to the doctor."

She chews her lip. "Are you sure?"

"Yeah." Just please don't take me to a doctor.

A deep sigh makes her chest rise, then fall. She seems

about to say something else, but changes her mind and instead caresses my face once more before standing. "Dinner will be ready in a few minutes. Are you well enough to eat?"

My stomach grumbles in response. "I'll be down in a minute."

Chapter 6

Turner picks up a piece of chalk and writes on the board as he speaks. "Your next assignment is to create a one-page sports section for the newspaper. You must photograph at least three sporting events and they must be accompanied by a one to two paragraph article."

Several groans rise up from the class, mine among the loudest.

"This is a photojournalism class. I realize most of you are in here for the photography aspect, but you do need to know how to string together a sentence or two, especially if it means the difference between your work getting published or not." He turns to face us and his eyes settle on mine. "You have ten days to work on this project and I can help you with the writing portion," he scans the room and smirks, "as long as you aren't calling me at home the Sunday night before it's due."

Several people laugh.

"We'll go over the details of the final project next week, but in the meantime, here's a list of all the games from today through next weekend." He hands a stack of papers to the person at the head of each row and returns to his desk. "I'm giving you two weekends since I know how busy your social lives are." He rolls his eyes. "But don't put it off until next weekend. Try to get at least one in tonight or tomorrow."

I glance down the list. Track. Ugh. Football. Also not my thing, but at least there will be lots of other people there. Soccer. Amelia has a crush on Trace so I'm sure she'd go to that with me. Maybe I can do two during the week and save football for next weekend.

The bell rings and students file past me.

"You doing anything after school?"

I startle at the deep voice next to me. "Cam, you scared me!" I grab my bag and we walk to the door. "Just homework, why?"

His dark hair falls over his forehead as we step into the hall. He seems to hesitate.

I stop. Since when does he not just spit out whatever he's thinking? "You okay?"

He turns to face me and rubs the back of his neck. The tendons in his forearm flex and my gaze flits to his bicep.

I shake my head. What the fuck?

"I thought maybe we could go for a drive or something."

"Sure," I say without understanding where this is going. We've gone for drives before, but it usually just happens. He's never actually asked me.

"Do you wanna meet by your car after class?" His eyes dart over my shoulder and he bites his lower lip. If I didn't know better, I'd swear he's nervous.

I reach out to touch his bare arm, but hesitate. My hand falls back to my side. "You sure you're okay?"

A small smile lifts the corner of his mouth as he watches my hand twitch at my side. "I could use a friend right now."

Right. Because we're friends. Something is seriously wrong with me today. "Yeah, but can we take your car?" I tap my forehead with my finger.

"Again?" His smile fades and my gut clenches. I don't need more people worrying about me. Especially Cameron. He has enough on his mind right now.

"I'll be fine. But it's probably better if you drive this afternoon."

Don't need to flicker in the middle of what looks like will be a serious conversation.

◆ ◆ ◆

The rest of the day drags—one more reason I don't want to flicker after school, especially on a Friday—and I'm already on my feet when the bell sounds.

Amelia's waiting at my locker. "You still coming over tonight?"

I shove my books in my bag and slip into my jacket. "Cam asked me to go for a drive." She raises an eyebrow and I hold my hands up in mock surrender. "I have no idea. I'm guessing he wants to talk about his sister."

"Then you definitely have to come over tonight. Besides, we need to plot how I can get Trace to notice me." Her eyes drift down the hall to where Trace's locker is. He has a game tonight and so is most likely already on a bus to whatever high school they're playing, but that doesn't stop her from looking for him.

"Have you talked to him?" Amelia is shy when it comes to meeting people, but once you get her talking it's impossible not to love her.

"I've smiled at him a couple times but he's always with a group of friends. I can't go up to him unless he's by himself."

I remember the list of games from photo class. I could do a feature on a player. And I'll need an assistant. "I might be able to help you there." She opens her mouth but I step backwards and laugh before she can ask. "I'll tell you about it tonight. Just have the popcorn ready."

◆ ◆ ◆

Cameron's car is easy to spot, and not because the parking lot is half empty by the time I get there—he's the only student brave enough to drive an orange car. He's not there yet so I climb onto Old Berta's hood and watch the leaves dance over the faded yellow lines.

This sudden shift in the way I'm reacting to him has me

off-balance. It's hard to miss the fact that he's hot. Besides his perfect arms and perfect hair, he's got long legs and strong hands and—

Jesus Christ, what is wrong with me? It's never been like that between us. Cameron's been in my life since we were kids. We're Cam and Biz. Friends. Nothing more.

"You look like you're arguing with yourself in your head."

I look up in surprise, my hands still waving in front of me, and my stomach flips. Cameron's standing a couple feet in front of me, his arms crossed over his chest and a full smile spread across his face. Oh yeah, he's got a killer smile, too.

"What's got you so worked up?"

"Worked up?" My voice squeaks and I blush. Stop it! It's just Cameron.

He cocks his head, pausing a beat before unlocking the passenger door. "I know we're here because I want to talk, but is there something you need to talk about?" His expression grows serious and he touches my arm. Electricity zings to my elbow.

I glance at his fingers resting lightly on my sleeve. Watch as he fingers the fabric. My mouth suddenly goes dry. What was the question?

"Biz?" he says, lowering his head until he's looking close into my eyes. "Are you okay? Is your headache that bad?"

I shake my head, wincing at the stabbing pains that protest the sudden movement. "No, sorry. I just lost my train of thought for a second." I move past him and climb into the car. Flashing a smile, I try to play off whatever the hell is going on inside me.

He pushes the door closed and lopes around to the driver's side.

Once we're on the road I force a couple deep breaths and risk a peek at Cam.

One hand is perched on the top of the steering wheel, the other on the gearshift—one more thing on the hotness meter—and he's watching me out of the corner of his eye. "I thought you were gonna pass out. Should I just take you home?"

I've passed out on him before, so it's a fair question. I slap my cheeks and roll my shoulders, making him laugh. "Nope, I'm good to go. No passing out here."

He smiles again, and his dimple winks at me. "Good."

We drive in silence until we reach the boat ramp near his house. A lot of kids party here at night, but right now it's deserted. He kills the engine but doesn't move.

I'm not sure if I'm supposed to say something or just wait him out. This uncertainty around Cameron is new to me and I feel like saying the wrong thing would undo whatever seems to be going on. After what feels like eons I open my mouth to speak, but snap it closed when he releases the steering wheel and folds his hands behind his head.

But he still doesn't say anything.

Can I get a clue for $200, Alex?

Cam exhales and leans his head against the seat so he's facing the top of the car.

"Cam?" My nervousness fades, replaced by my earlier concern. "If you don't want to talk about it, we can just hang out here. Or do you wanna go sit by the water?"

He lowers his gaze and stares out at the lake. Ripples break the surface, sending flashes of light bouncing into my skull. "Yeah."

We slam the doors behind us and crunch over the gravel towards the water's edge.

He touches my jacket then glances down at his bare arms, as if realizing for the first time that he wasn't wearing a coat. "I think I have a blanket in the trunk. Hold on."

And the butterflies are back.

"Sorry for dragging you all the way out here to talk." Cam spreads out the blanket and I sit on one side. He leans back on his hands, his legs stretched out in front of him.

"You know you don't need to apologize to me." I pull my knees tightly against my chest and wrap my arms around them. Whatever has shifted inside me seems to have a mind of its own and I don't want to risk doing something stupid when Cam clearly just wants to talk.

"You've probably figured out that this whole kidnapping thing is hitting me hard."

So that is what this is about. But being right doesn't make me feel as good as it normally does. Instead I feel worse.

"I don't know if it's the fact that they're the same age, or what, but I haven't been able to think of anything but Katie since yesterday." His voice breaks when he says his little sister's name.

I fight the urge to touch him, to comfort him somehow. "I've been thinking about her too."

He faces me. "You have?"

"Well yeah. It'd be impossible not to. I remember how awful it was. I've been worried about how this was affecting you."

His lips tighten in a firm line and he stares straight ahead at the water.

I really don't want to make him cry, but I can't exactly change the topic. "What have your parents said?"

"Not much. It's been really quiet at home, like we're all afraid to say her name."

"You shouldn't have to do that."

"What else are we supposed to do? It's not like we have a grave we can visit when we're feeling sad. My mom finally put away her toys and stuff but her room is still her room." He leans forward and pulls his legs towards his body. "It's like we're still waiting for her to come home."

I want to ask if the police have contacted him, but I'm afraid to go there. Instead I let my hand drift towards his. We've never actually held hands before, but I don't know what else to do.

His head jerks towards me, then his eyes drop to our hands. He doesn't move for several seconds. I'm about to pull away when he laces his fingers through mine. His warmth seeps through my skin and it's as if he's heating my entire body through the palm of my hand.

"Can I do anything?"

His other hand covers mine and the hurt lifts from his eyes. "You being here is all I wanted."

I can't tear my eyes away from his mouth. How have I never noticed his lips before? The fact that he's sitting much closer than he normally does and for the first time in a long time we're both single might have something to do with it. Not that he's thinking about that right now. I close my eyes, still not quite believing Cam is the one holding my hand and making me want to be kissed more than I ever have before.

A car horn blasts in the parking lot and we both jump. Embarrassed, I pull my hand from his, but Cameron seems unaware of what I'm thinking and continues to watch the river in silence.

Laughter erupts behind us as a group of our classmates get out of the car. "Sorry to interrupt!" one of them shouts, and more giggles follow.

Cam shakes his head. "Do you want to get out of here?"

"Only if you do. It'll be hard to talk with them right there." Even though talking is hardly what I'd like to be doing. And that definitely can't be done with them ten feet away.

Cam answers me by standing. He holds out a hand to help me up.

I slip my hand into his and I get another jolt.

He pulls me to my feet. "What are you doing later?"

"Going to Amelia's to watch movies." And talk about you. He drops my hand to pick up the blanket and I start walking to the car. I'd rather stay with him, but considering how well I seem to be doing with guys lately, maybe it's better that nothing actually happened. I'd hate to jeopardize our friendship for a quick make-out session.

If only I believed that.

◆ ◆ ◆

Cam turns on his mp3 player and the latest FloMo song fills the car.

I cast a sidelong look at him. He knows she's my favorite singer, but did he play it on purpose or was that just what came next in his playlist? And why am I suddenly so obsessed over this? An exasperated sigh rushes past my lips. It's pretty bad when you're annoying yourself.

Cam seems unaffected by whatever happened at the lake. Maybe it's all in my head. I know he's thinking about his sister, and I'm a little jealous that he can turn off those emotions so easily. Not that I'm envious of what he's thinking about.

Okay, seriously. I need to just shut up.

"You're doing it again."

My head whips at him. "Doing what?"

"Arguing with yourself."

I blush.

"Are you going to tell me what's you're so frustrated about?"

I think fast. "Just our assignment for class. I figure I'll go to the football game next week, and probably a soccer game with Amelia, but I'm not sure about the third." I rub my hands over my thighs to dry the sweat that's suddenly seeping from every pore in my body. "What ones are you going to?"

"Probably football. And maybe soccer." My stomach flips. "Do you want to go to the third one together?"

I smile. "You mean once we know which one it is?"

He slows as the car in front of us makes a turn. "I figure track'll be easy."

Dammit! I wasn't paying attention to where we're going

and now we're practically to the Strand. I close my eyes and hope he doesn't notice.

"Plus we can probably get pretty close to the runners. Not like with the sports that play on a field."

My hand slides over my eyes and I force a deep breath. Nothing's tingling, but freaking myself out makes it hard to tell if I'm going to flicker.

"I think there's a meet on Tuesday."

I don't want to, but I lean forward. Cam wouldn't know if I flicker, and it wouldn't be all bad to repeat today, but I don't want this moment to end. We'll be past it in another minute, then everything will be fine.

"Biz?"

Crap.

"What the hell? Why didn't you tell me?" His hand is so light on the back of my head I can hardly tell he's touching me. The car slows and I sit up straight.

"No, don't stop. I'll be fine in a minute."

"How can you be fine in a minute? I'm pulling over."

Stopping in the Strand doesn't mean I'll automatically flicker. When we're stopped it's just like being anyplace else.

But eventually we'll have to start up again.

Gravel crunches as the car rolls to a stop. I open my eyes and take a quick breath. Cam is leaning close, his dark eyes just inches from mine.

This probably wouldn't be the best time to kiss him.

"You're freaking me out. Are you sure you don't need help?"

"Cam, how many times have I told you? My headaches… they come and go. I know it seems weird but I've learned to live with them." I will a smile to my lips. My head is ready to split in two, but I'm not lying about learning to deal with the headaches. They're a part of my life and I can either hide in my bedroom or live my life.

His hand lowers to the back of my neck and I mentally beg him to rub out the knots. Yeah, I was all nerves two seconds ago, but I become a massage whore when a migraine's got a hold of me. I don't care who you are; if you'll make the pain go away—even for a couple minutes—I'll love you forever.

His fingers trace the bumps of my spine, a gesture that would have turned me into a puddle if I wasn't so focused on making the pain go away.

"Cam, I'm okay. I swear." I reach up and place my hand over

his, but my telepathy fails and he lowers our hands until they're resting on the edge of my seat.

"I wish I knew what was going on inside your head."

You and me both.

He turns my hand over, his thumb rubbing small circles on the back of my hand. "I guess sitting here doesn't really do much if you do need help. You sure you just want to go home?"

"Yeah." I don't, but I really should lie down before going over to Amelia's house. Something tells me it's going to be a long night.

He tries to hold my hand for the rest of the drive, but the stick makes it difficult. After the third attempt we both start laughing, and whatever weirdness may have hovered between us is left at the Strand.

My nerves slam into me all over again when we pull into my driveway. He seems to be working up the nerve to say something, but I cut him off with a quick kiss on the cheek. "Call me tomorrow and we'll figure out the other game."

A hint of color floods his cheeks. "I will."

I bounce from the car happier than I've been in a long time. Even before Robbie. Maybe things are finally picking up for me.

Chapter 7

I open the front door and freeze. From the kitchen I hear a spastic knocking, like something's hitting one of the chairs and making it scrape across the tile floor.

"Dad!"

My mother's voice murmurs over the banging.

I sprint to the kitchen.

My dad's sprawled on the floor, seizing, his legs slamming into a chair with each uncontrolled convulsion. Mom's cross-legged on the floor with his head loosely cradled in her lap, the phone wedged against her shoulder.

My body reacts without thinking. I kick the chair across the room and lightly grip his ankles. Restraining him is pointless; I just want to keep him from hurting himself.

"Biz, this one's bad. Be care—"

A violent spasm grips his leg and his slippered foot catches me in the chin.

I fall backwards, stunned.

Everything goes dark and the only sound is a low hum coming from deep inside my head. Then the headache rages forward and the room clears.

"Are you okay?" The phone clatters to the floor, forgotten.

That's a first. I reach for Dad's feet but this time I throw my legs over his. "Yeah, I'm great."

"An ambulance is on the way. Maybe they should check you out while we're there."

"An ambulance?" I choose to ignore the second thing she said. I'm not letting them near my head any sooner than I have to. The spasms seem to have slowed, but I'm so used to this sometimes it's hard to tell.

"He hit his head when he fell. I was in the other room."

For the first time I notice my mom's disheveled appearance. Her normally smooth hair is sticking all over the place and fresh tears streak her face, smudging her makeup. Brightly painted shards of pottery speckle the floor around her.

The pill bowl.

"Why didn't you call me?"

"I called the hospital first. You were next."

Of course. How selfish can I be?

We remain like that until uniformed men flood the kitchen. They wrap one of those collar things around Dad's neck, strap him to a gurney, then wheel him from the house.

I grab my phone. "Can you drive?" I definitely don't want to relive this.

We follow the ambulance through the neighborhood past rows and rows of trees, all standing straight and proud and ready to fuck with my head.

"Shit."

"Biz."

"Sorry. I left my sunglasses in my car." Yes, I could look the other way, but it's the inconvenience that irritates me.

She fumbles in the center console and hands me a pair of oversized shades.

"Thanks."

"Are you sure you won't let them examine you?"

I can feel her watching me. "I'm getting tired of always having to convince everyone that I'm okay. Yes, I get headaches but there are worse things in the world." I nod at the ambulance in front of us.

Her lips set in a firm line. I pushed too far.

"I'm sorry mom. I know you're worried. But please stop worrying about me."

We don't speak again until we arrive at the hospital, where we're faced with a kaleidoscope of lights bouncing off the bright white walls of the emergency entrance. Pinpricks shoot from the tips of my fingers straight up my arms. Same thing in my feet. The heaviness slams into me. This is much faster than with the sunlight. My only comfort is knowing that artificial light can't make me flicker. I only feel everything else.

Mom knows light affects me, but she only knows about the headaches. But this is so severe I'm not sure if I can pretend that nothing is happening.

I stumble as we pass by the ambulance that ferried my dad and a strong hand grips my arm, keeping me on my feet. A pair of eyes I've never seen appear.

"Are you all right?"

For the love of god, would people please stop asking me that? I nod dumbly. I don't think I'm very convincing because he guides me to the back of the open ambulance and sits me on the bumper.

Now Mom is hovering behind his shoulder, her lower lip caught between her teeth. Her eyes dart between me and the entrance to the hospital.

"Mom, go with Dad. I'll be there in a minute. I just got dizzy." I blink hard and when I open my eyes, she's gone. A small part of me wishes she hadn't listened, but then I'd just be bitching that she worries too much. I focus on the man still kneeling in front of me. "Thanks for catching me. I've had a migraine for a couple days and I guess it just caught up with me."

He's still holding my arms. "I'm choosing to believe you, even though I get the feeling it's more than just a migraine."

I take a second look at him. He's older than me but much younger than my parents, and way more filled out than the guys at school. At first glance I figured him for the guy who drove the ambulance, but—

He smiles. "I've got a thing for neurology."

An urge to flee zips through me. "That sounds cool." Swallowing hard, I force a smile. There's no way this guy knows anything. I push to my feet and he takes a step back.

"I didn't mean to upset you."

I glance at his name tag. Martinez. "You didn't. You're just doing your job." I nod at the entrance. "I gotta go see my dad." I rush through the automatic door and glance over my shoulder.

He's still watching me.

◆ ◆ ◆

The nurse at the front desk smiles when she sees me. "They're working on him now. Your mom's already in the waiting room."

"Thanks." I move on auto-pilot; past the desk, past the swinging doors where doctors put people back together, and through the glass doors to the waiting room. Although it's Friday, it's still early and there aren't many people here. A couple huddle together on the only sofa, and a woman with two little kids is camped in the chairs near the TV. Mom is standing near the floor-length window, her back to the room, no doubt trying to pretend we aren't in the hospital.

Again.

I approach her cautiously. Now that Dad's with the doctors, whatever check she had on her emotions is about to come unhinged. "Did they say anything?"

She faces me. Her mascara has finished its transition from her lashes to her cheeks and her lower lip is bleeding.

I wrap an arm around her. "Mom, he'll be okay." I want to believe that. I have to. They say teenagers believe they're invincible, but I think it goes beyond that. Parents are invincible too. Because what happens if something happens to them?

"They think he fractured his skull when he fell. They won't know for sure until they get the X-rays back, which should be," she checks her watch, "in another ten minutes or so. I just hope to god he doesn't need surgery." She turns away from the window and drops into the nearest chair with her head in her hands.

The couple on the couch watch us for a moment before pressing their foreheads together again.

I don't know what to say. I want to reassure her, but A, I don't know that he'll be okay, and B, I figure the less I talk the more she'll stay focused on Dad and not remember that she wants me to get my head looked at. I'm tempted to feel my chin to see if it's bruising, but I may as well set off a flare. If there was a bruise she would have said something by now.

My beeping cell phone yanks me out of my reverie and I silence it. I go to my texts. Amelia wants to know when I'll be over.

"Sorry. Dad's in hospital. Maybe tomorrow?" I text back.

I fall into the chair next to Mom and wait for her reply.

Mom straightens in her seat. "You don't need to wait here. I'll be all right if you want to go outside and make a call."

"Are you sure? What if they come back with news?"

"Then I'll come get you. Just stay where I can see you from the doors."

I hesitate. Yeah, I want to talk to Amelia, but despite what I said I really am worried about Dad. Mom doesn't hold her shit together very well when she's by herself. "Do you promise to come get me?"

She nods, but her eyes are already glazed over.

I kiss her cheek, then head for the exit, stopping at the main desk. "I'm going outside, but will you make sure someone gets me if anything happens with my dad? My mom..." I hate to talk bad about her, but they know.

The nurse smiles for the second time since I've been there. "Of course."

Chapter 8

Technically the low wall alongside the area where the ambulances drop off patients isn't a waiting area, but no one's ever yelled at me. Amelia still hasn't texted back, so I call her.

"Hey, is your dad okay? It's been awhile since he's had to go to the hospital, right?"

"Yeah, not since last winter." That day played out much the same way, except there was two feet of snow and our car spun into a ditch. That's probably why Mom called the ambulance this time.

"So... how is this one different?" Amelia doesn't like to pry—that's one of the things I love about her—but it's a fair question. Usually Dad's seizures are pretty mild and we just ride them out at home.

"They think he cracked his skull when he fell." I touch my chin. "Then I caught a foot in the face. That was fantastic."

She gasps. "Is your mom freaking out?"

I snort. "What do you think?" Guilt pricks me and I look down at the ground. "I can't blame her though. Every time is scary, even the mild ones."

There's a pause and I realize Amelia doesn't know what to say.

I clear my throat. "So do you want to hear my plan?"

A breathy chuckle erupts through the phone. "I thought you'd never ask! Tell me, how do you plan to get Trace to notice me?"

"Well," I say, drawing it out, "my latest photo assignment is to put together a fake sports page for the school paper. I figure I'll take pictures of the soccer game, then ask Trace if I can interview him." Never mind the fact that I've never interviewed anyone in my life. This is what you do for friends. "You, naturally, will be my assistant."

There's a thump and I can hear her clap her hands. "I love it!" she shouts, her voice miles away. There's rustling, then her voice is clearer. "Sorry, the phone kinda shot out from under my chin. Do you think that'll work?"

"I hadn't considered that it wouldn't. What guy–especially a jock–doesn't like to talk about himself?"

"Biz, that's awesome! So when are we going?"

"I think there's a game on Tuesday. But you need to help me come up with questions. You know I'm no good at that kind of stuff." She giggles and I roll my eyes. "And nothing about his abs or his legs!"

"Oh, come on!"

I laugh again and an EMT glances at me. I mouth 'sorry' and shift so I'm facing away from him. I want to tell her about Cameron, but part of me hesitates. If I say it out loud it'll be real and then it's only a matter of time before it all goes to shit.

"Speaking of super hot boys..." Amelia prompts.

"It's like you fricking read my mind sometimes, you know?"

"That's why I'm your best friend. Spill it. Did he want to talk about his sister?"

I'm sure we talked about his sister, but the first thing I remember is how badly I wanted to kiss him. I touch my lips.

"Helloooo?"

I shake my head. "He brought her up, but we didn't really talk much."

"Oh?" The innuendo in her voice nearly topples me over.

"What?"

"I've seen the way he looks at you. I figured now that you dumped Robbie things might happen with you two."

Heat shoots through me. Maybe it wasn't in my head. "Where the hell have I been during all this?"

"I don't know. When you told me you were going for a drive with him I assumed you liked him." She pauses. "Do you like him?"

Cameron's muscular arms flash through my mind, followed by his smile, his legs, and those lips.

"Ha, I knew it!"

"But what if I screw everything up? I don't want to lose him as a friend."

"Biz, as your younger and less experienced friend, I have to tell you that sometimes that's a risk you have to take."

Younger my ass. I'm only two weeks older. "Did you read that at inspirational-poems-dot-com?"

She snorts. "Close. Turning-your-friend-into-a-lover-dot-net."

I burst out laughing and my face burns. Kissing was as far as I'd allowed my imagination to go, but a rush of images floods my head and now I can't think straight.

Which works out well because the smiley nurse is heading my way.

"Amelia, I gotta go."

"Okay. Call me later."

I disconnect and meet the nurse in the center of the ambulance bay. "Is he okay?"

She guides me back to where I'd been standing. "They've finished examining him and would like to keep him overnight for observation. There's a small fracture in the back of his skull but it doesn't look like there's any serious damage."

I look at the doors.

"The doctor already talked to your mom. She wants to stay here, although there really isn't any need. Do you have a way home, or do you have anyone you can call to stay with you?"

I bristle, then immediately chastise myself. She's just trying to be nice. "I'll need to find a ride home, but I'm fine by myself."

She looks around. "You know, I bet Rick can drop you off. I'll radio him and find out where he's at."

"Rick?"

"Martinez. The EMT who brought your dad in."

"I don't know…"

She dismisses my concern with a wave of her hand. "He's completely harmless. I bet he'll let you play with the lights if you ask nicely."

That's so not where I was going with that, but there's no sense arguing. I need a ride home and apparently this Rick will do whatever she asks. If only I had a tinfoil hat for the ride home. "Let me make sure my mom's okay with me leaving."

"Your dad's in room 214. I'll come get you when Rick is here."

Great.

I trudge up the stairs to the second floor, digging deep for the energy to comfort Mom.

She's sitting in a plastic chair pulled tight against the bed. A fluorescent light flickers over Dad's bandaged head, the blue-white impulses casting long shadows around the room as he sleeps. Or lies there unconscious.

I knock lightly on the door before entering. "Mom, can I get you anything? Have you eaten?" I know she won't—not while my dad is like this—but I can't not offer.

She looks up as if surprised to see me. The mascara's been wiped from her face, revealing red puffy skin that threatens to close her eyes. "No, I'm fine. I'll just wait here with your father."

My eyes close against the harsh lights, but the stabbing near my ear remains. I take a deep breath. "The nurse said you're gonna stay here?"

She murmurs softly, but I can't tell if she's answering me or talking to Dad.

"Mom?"

"You go on home, dear. There's no sense in us both staying."

I tell myself she's a little concerned with how I'll get home, or the fact that I'll be staying home alone. I mean, I could have a party and trash the house. I back away towards the hall.

"Biz?" Mom lifts her head, her glassy eyes on me.

My hand rests on the doorknob.

"Please be careful. I know you don't want the doctors looking at you, but I haven't forgotten what happened."

My chest tightens. I give her a small smile. "I will, Mom."

◆ ◆ ◆

Rick is leaning against the ambulance when I walk outside. "Samantha says you need a ride home."

Something about the way he's standing—one foot propped against the ambulance, his arms crossed over his chest—makes me uncomfortable. Earlier I hadn't really looked at him, but now that it's just the two of us out here I'm suddenly aware of how... male... he is. Strong arms, with tendons twisting to his wrists, ending at hands could crush my head. I'm not sure whether to be frightened or—

"So, do you?"

My hand snakes to the back of my neck and squeezes. I can't think straight with this stupid headache. "Yeah, thanks."

"Well hop on in." He shoves away from the ambulance with his foot and opens the passenger door in one fluid movement.

I move past him, suddenly self-conscious. I've never been inside an ambulance before. For the most part it looks like a regular truck, just bigger and with a lot more buttons. Not to mention the computer. A row of switches on the ceiling catch my attention.

"You can flip 'em on once we're on the road. Most kids

think it's fun."

I scowl at him. "I'm not twelve."

He holds up his hands. "Hey, I don't know. I'm doing Samantha a favor and thought I'd try to be nice." He guns the engine and we roll away from the hospital.

Dusk has settled and neon lights blink all around us. My eyes close out of habit. I'm about to ask him how he knows where we're going when I remember he was already at my house. My thoughts flit to Dad and I sink back in the seat. Maybe I shouldn't have left.

"You sure it's just a headache that's affecting you?"

I raise an eyebrow without opening my eyes. "Why do you ask?"

Based on the length of his pause, he's considering his answer carefully. "Like I said, I'm into neurology and the way your pupils were all over the place..." He shakes his head.

My pupils? This is new to me. I open one eye. "What were they dilated or something?"

He glances at me, his eyes bright with curiosity. "One of them was."

Excuses leap to my lips, but I keep them to myself. I get the feeling he already knows it's all bullshit.

"I don't know what's going on with you, but you should really get it checked out. You don't want to find out too late that you have something seriously wrong with your brain. It's not like pulling a muscle or breaking a bone. Once your brain goes haywire it's a lot harder to fix."

Fantastic.

"I'm not trying to scare you. At least, not too much, but you seem like a smart kid," he smirks. "I'm sorry, young woman. And I'd hate for you to waste that because you're skittish around MDs."

"Who are you?" The words fly from my mouth before I can stop them. "I mean…" I'm more shocked than pissed but I can't backtrack now. "You meet me for two seconds and you think you can analyze me? Don't they have patients at the hospital for you to play around with?"

His jaw clenches. His hard eyes meet mine. "Yeah, they do. But the ones with these problems are already dead."

That shuts me up.

"Look, I'm sorry. I'm not trying to be a jerk. If you say you're fine I guess I have to accept that. But will you promise me one thing?"

"Sure. Because I make promises to strangers all the time."

"If whatever is wrong with you gets worse, will you tell someone?"

I turn away, unable to bear the intensity of his gaze. He'd be a good doctor if he's this passionate about every person he encounters.

The streetlights on my block are on, but my house is dark. He pulls into the driveway. "You didn't answer."

"I know."

"Okay, at the very least, don't forget what I've said. I guess that's all I can really hope for."

I smile at him, but my lips feel lopsided. "That I can do." I open the door and jump down to the driveway. "Thanks for the ride."

He nods and waits in the driveway, the ambulance idling, until I've let myself into the house.

Inside, I check every room, lock every door and window, and turn on every light. I put a frozen dinner in the microwave and lean on the counter while it cooks.

I text Amelia to say hi, then Cameron, then continue to wait.

Three minutes later the microwave beeps but neither of them have texted back. I bring my food to my bedroom, stopping by the bathroom to grab my medicine, then flop onto my bed with the stereo blasting.

Some Friday night.

Chapter 9

A slamming door wakes me up. Faint sunlight streams through my curtains. What time is it?

I slowly sit up, flinching in anticipation of the daggers that are ready to pierce my brain, but they remain sheathed. I gingerly poke my chin and wince. Seems the daggers have relocated there.

"Biz?" Mom calls from downstairs.

"In my room." I reach for the glass of water on my nightstand and pause, my hand in midair. The plastic dish from last night's dinner is flipped upside-down on the floor, cheese and pasta oozing from beneath it, completely crusted to the carpet.

Mom sighs in the doorway.

"At least my headache's gone." I smile my best 'aww-shucks' grin and rap my knuckles against my skull. Lightly. "Did they release Dad?"

She crosses her arm over her chest so her hand settles on her shoulder, as if she's holding herself together. "Not for a couple more hours. His doctor is doing rounds and will see him after that."

I'm surprised she left.

"I'm sorry I—" her eyes drift closed. The remorse plays out on her features before it leaves her mouth. Tightly clenched lips, crows feet deeper than usual, flexing her fist.

I save her the trouble. "I know Mom. You were worried about Dad. I was too."

"But that doesn't excuse me from looking out for you. It didn't occur to me until the middle of the night that I had no idea how you got home."

Sometimes I wish she'd keep these things to herself. It's how she copes, I know that, but it just reinforces the fact that I'm not the most important person to her.

"So?" She's watching me now.

"The ambulance driver drove me."

She raises an eyebrow. I can tell she wants to say more, but she's the one who put me in that position and prolonging this conversation will only make her feel worse.

"Well I'm glad you're feeling better. Will you be around today?"

That's a good question. My phone beckons, but I hold off. "I'm not sure. I'll stick around until Dad gets home. Maybe get started on some homework."

This seems to please her. "I'll go make breakfast." She eyes my spoiled dinner. "You must be hungry."

I wait until I hear pots banging before calling Amelia.

"How's your dad?"

"Still in the hospital, but supposedly coming home soon. What'd I miss last night?"

There's a rustle of fabric, followed by the squeak of bedsprings. "I ended up at the mall and saw Trace. We didn't talk or anything, but I'm pretty sure he looked at me."

I laugh. "Looked at you? What, did you run by screaming or something?" I wouldn't put it past her to create a scene just to get his attention. A minor scene, but a scene nonetheless.

She huffs. "I'm not that bad. I just made sure we crossed paths. Several—well, maybe a dozen times."

"Subtle."

"Hey, it made him look at me. Don't they say any publicity is good publicity?"

"Yeah, unless he thinks you're a freak. Just don't scare him off before the game on Tuesday, otherwise my plan won't work."

"Do you really think he'll go for it?"

"You know him better than me, but I think so. Especially if I take a bunch of pictures of him. I don't think we have to submit the project to the paper, but I can promise him I will."

"Biz, you rock."

"Yeah, yeah. I still haven't figured out what other game to go to."

"Too bad the swim team doesn't start until next semester. That could make for a hot spread." She bursts out laughing and I roll my eyes, smiling.

My phone vibrates in my hand and I check the display. A text from Cameron. "Speaking of hot…"

Amelia snorts.

"Give me a call if you decide to do anything."

"Tell Cam hello."

I read Cameron's text. "No games today. Wanna hang out?"

This text is no different from any other I've received from him, but my heart seems to think it's a sonnet from Shakespeare. I take a deep breath and text back. "Love to. Later today?" I meant what I said to Mom about staying here until Dad comes home. I need to see for myself that he's okay.

"Pick you up at four?"

That could almost be a date. Is it a date? Now I'm gonna have to call Amelia back. "See you then."

I peel myself out of bed and cheese squishes between my toes. "Ew!" I jump in the air, landing on my trig book. "Well that seems fitting." I grab a random sock and wipe off my foot before heading downstairs in search of something to clean the carpet.

I must really like Cameron. No one's ever had me so distracted that I've stepped in my dinner.

◆ ◆ ◆

I'm passed out on the couch when my parents get home. My

big plans to study gave way to a movie marathon, which gave way to a nap. I sit up as they come inside.

Dad's head is bandage-free and the two-inch gash on the back of his skull gives me a gnarly smile.

"Holy crap! That's just from hitting the floor?" I rush to his side and lightly touch the stitches, then give him a hug. He rubs my back, up and down, like he did when I was little. I turn to Mom. "There wasn't any blood on the floor."

She glances at her pants. "Most of it was on me."

Now I feel like a shit. I've been so pouty about being the poor neglected child that I failed to notice Dad's blood all over her.

Dad touches my chin and lifts my face so I'm looking at him. His brow furrows. "I hear I knocked you a good one." His thumb runs over the tip of my chin and I try not to flinch. What he's gone through is so much worse than getting kicked in the face.

I shrug. "I'll be okay. Everything happened so fast that I didn't have much time to think about it."

He doesn't say anything at first, just looks at me with a curious expression on his face.

Mom clears her throat. "I'll let you two catch up. Are sandwiches okay for lunch?"

We both nod, still looking at each other. He walks to the couch and lowers himself carefully, first gripping the back, then the armrest, then falling awkwardly onto the cushions.

"Why don't you let me help you?"

He ignores me. "What else happened?"

"What do you mean?"

"I can tell your mind's going a thousand miles a minute, and it's not about this latest case of child abuse."

I smile despite myself. When I was seven he clocked me in the side of the head during a seizure and an overly-protective substitute teacher alerted the school that she suspected I was being abused at home. It's happened countless times over the years—the accidental injuries, not the reports of abuse—and the joke helps lessen his anguish over hurting me.

"One kind of weird thing happened, but… I don't know." Why did I even bring that up? Dad's pretty cool about not insisting I see a doctor, but I may not be able to hold them off much longer.

He leans his head back, in no hurry. I think they teach

that in advanced parenting classes, the ones I'm convinced my parents snuck off to when they said they were playing mah jongg. I can't stand for there to be silence between us. And he, of course, knows this.

I sigh dramatically and flop onto the couch next to him. "One of the ambulance drivers kinda weirded me out." Rick's intense gaze flashed through my mind.

Dad visibly tenses.

"Nothing like that. I tripped when we were going into the hospital and he went on and on about how he's into neurology." Shut up, Biz. "I think he was just trying to impress me." Or find a pet project.

"So he didn't do anything inappropriate? He just talked about… your headaches?"

"Pretty much." Maybe it's best I don't tell him that Rick drove me home and basically scared the bejeebers out of me.

His heavy sigh makes me turn to face him.

The sutures peek out from the couch cushion and my stomach clenches. Suddenly he seems very fragile. Despite his illness, Dad's the rock in our family. We revolve around him and, in turn, he holds us together. I fear that without him

Mom and I would flounder, aimlessly drifting though life in his absence.

His eyelids flutter. I hope it's just the drugs. "Will you promise me something?"

"Uh, sure?"

"If there's ever something… more, with your headaches. Even if it seems like I'd never understand. Will you tell me?"

All the times I've flickered streak by like a movie—the tingling, the heaviness, the sudden jerk when I come to—followed by the memory of the crushing pain afterwards. How could he ever understand that?

"Of course."

Chapter 10

It's quarter to four. I'm wearing my favorite sweater, my favorite shoes, and the jeans that make my ass look as good as it's going to get. Now I just need to figure out who or what's possessed me and I'll happily get on with my day.

I can't remember the last time I've acted this way over a boy.

My phone vibrates a couple minutes later. "I'm here."

Well at least he's early too.

I run upstairs to tell Mom and Dad I'm leaving and find them curled around each other on the bed, Mom's hands cradling Dad's head to her chest, his leg is thrown over hers. I hurry downstairs and leave a note on the kitchen counter letting them know I'm going out for the night. They know I always have my phone so they're pretty cool about letting me do my own thing. As long as I'm home on time, of course.

I step onto the front porch and lock the door behind me. When I face the street a brilliant light makes me shield my eyes so I don't see Cameron right away.

He's standing next to his car, seeming uncertain about whether or not to approach.

"What's up?"

"I was gonna come to the door, but then it seemed weird so I wasn't sure if I should just wait in the car."

My chest swells. I've known Cameron for too long for either of us to try to pretend to be something we're not. If one of us is nervous, the other one knows. I walk to the passenger side and open the door.

He catches my eye over the roof and my hands start to sweat. "I figured we'd meet up with everyone at the boat ramp later, but is there something you want to do right now?"

Do not say what just came to mind. I'm sure I'm blushing, but I hope the afternoon sun is giving me a healthy glow instead of the mottled flush that's probably covering my face.

"Biz?" He pauses, his arm resting on the open door.

I cock my head.

His face droops. "You haven't said a word since you came outside. Are you sure you want to hang out?"

"Oh god, yes! I'm sorry, I guess I'm just a little nervous."

He dips his head so his hair falls in his face and I can't see his eyes. "Okay, good."

We climb in and he backs out of my driveway, his hand wrapped firmly around the gearshift. It's probably best if we don't try to hold hands again, but my body aches to feel his touch.

"So where to?"

I lean my head on the seat. "Anywhere." The stress from the past day seeps out of me and a feeling of euphoria settles into my bones. Yes, I get this feeling every time a migraine goes away, but my proximity to Cameron has set off some kind of chemical reaction that's making it hard to worry about anything else.

"How about the zoo? I think it's open for a couple more hours."

I flinch, remembering that time years ago with Dad.

The first time I remember Dad having a seizure I was three years old. The three of us were at the zoo and halfway through the monkey house when he collapsed. I remember Mom standing over him, screaming. And the monkeys screaming back at her. Me—I couldn't tear my eyes away from the way the sunlight poured through an oblong skylight at the very top of the high ceiling and blanketed my father's twitching body. His arms flopped at his side. His legs kicked at nothing. And his eyes… that was the weirdest part. His eyes rolled around in his head until the color was gone and all I could see was white.

I never told Cameron about it and he doesn't notice my reaction. "That's cool." As long as we stay away from the monkey house.

Cam turns up the stereo and we ride through town, comfortable enough with each other to not need to ask a million questions or worry that they would rather be someplace else.

My eyes drift closed. Without the distraction of everything around us, I can hear him breathing. A flood of emotions overwhelm me at the thought of being this close to another person, even without touching, and I allow myself a moment to let my heart go crazy and wish for things I don't deserve.

Twenty minutes later, the car bumps over a curb and the engine cuts off. "We're here."

I open my eyes and jump. The largest tree I've ever seen is less than a foot in front of the car, its large branches shading us from the suns slanting rays. This isn't the zoo. "Where's here?"

Cameron stretches his arm across the space between the seats and lightly runs his fingers through my hair. A purr builds in my throat, but I control myself. He nods at a fence beyond the tree. "The zoo."

"I've lived here my entire life but I didn't know you could drive up to the back. Isn't there a big wall or something that keeps people from climbing the fence?"

"This isn't the edge of a cage. I think it's an outer perimeter that marks the edge of the property. I come here sometimes when I'm feeling trapped, like I can't find a way out of my bullshit life, you know?"

I peer at the wall. "That makes sense. Seeing creatures that really don't have any way out can make you feel better."

A sad smile touches his lips. "Exactly."

I pick at the edge of my seat. I can almost feel Katie sitting here with us. "Do you want to talk about her?"

He shifts forward so his forearms are crossed on the steering wheel, then rests his chin on his arms. "I don't know what to say. Nothing's changed. It's like we're back four years ago when she first disappeared. Wondering what if…"

Cameron had been the last one to see Katie. I'll never forget the crack in his voice when he told me. They'd been playing in the backyard while their mom was doing laundry and Katie ran around to the front to get her bike. He was so wrapped up in testing his new bike ramp that he just didn't realize how much time had passed. That she was still gone. By the time he went to see what was taking her so long, she'd vanished. Her bike lay at the end of the driveway, the pink tassels torn loose from the handlebars.

He called me first, desperate, not knowing what to do. I rode my bike to his house as fast as I could and got there minutes before the police arrived. They assumed I'd been there all along and neither of us corrected them—at least not until the questions started. The police eventually believed that Cam had nothing to do with her disappearance, but people have never looked at him the same.

A blue plastic barrette was found in the gutter and he still carries it with him as a reminder of that day.

I touch his arm.

He turns his head so his cheek is resting on his wrist, and our eyes meet.

"It's not your fault. There's no way—"

"I was supposed to be watching her. I was thirteen years old for fuck's sake, not some little kid." He sits upright and slams the heel of his hand into the steering wheel. The horn blasts and we both jump. "Sorry."

"Do you want to walk around? Get some air?"

"Sure."

We climb out and walk towards the fence, but I don't see a way in. He seems to know where he's going but if he's planning to climb the fence... I glance at my cute, but-not-very-practical-for-climbing-a-fence, shoes. "I don't know if I can climb—"

He grabs my hand. "We're not climbing the fence. There's a gate over here that isn't always locked." I reel back and he squeezes my hand. "It lets in behind a maintenance building and goes to the main part where people walk around. No tigers." He lifts my hand and brushes his lips over my knuckles.

Who am I kidding? I'd follow him through the lion's den

if he asked.

The gate is unlocked, but very loud. I cringe as he pries it open. We stop next to the low cinderblock building. "Are you sure we won't get in trouble?"

A mischievous grin chases away the pain that was there moments earlier. "Not really." He closes the gate and we peek around the corner. Families with strollers walk beneath the shady trees, and an elderly couple sits on a bench near the duck pond. "Ready?"

I squeeze his hand and he tugs me around the corner of the building. We swing our joined arms, not a care in the world, when a shout makes us both turn.

"Hey!"

We look at each other, eyes wide, then break into a run.

He leads me past a fountain, where I narrowly avoid slamming into a girl toddling behind a wagon. "Sorry!" I shout over my shoulder.

Cameron grabs my hand and tugs me off the path and behind a clump of bushes. We fall to the ground, elbows and knees colliding, and burst out laughing.

"Do you think he's still after us?" I didn't look back while we were running but our escape was hardly well thought out.

He sits up and pulls apart the branches. "Doesn't look like it."

I swat his arm. "You can't even see."

"True, but if he was looking for us he'd already be here." He turns to face me. "I think we're safe."

My adrenaline slows, but my senses are still humming.

Cameron slides closer.

Our eyes meet, and everything else fades away. The kids screaming for the ducks, the gravel crunching beneath the strollers—the only thing in my universe is him.

"Come here," he whispers as he lowers his head towards mine.

My stomach backflips. I tear my eyes away from his lips to search his eyes, see the same excitement that I feel. I take an unsteady breath and lean into his kiss.

Any concern I had about ruining our friendship vanishes as his strong arms wrap around me. His lips are firmer than I expected, and more insistent. My hands slide up his back and into the soft hair at the base of his neck.

A small sigh escapes him and his lips part, his warm tongue gently touching mine.

I move still closer, until I'm tucked against him, safe from everything around us. No light, no tests, just the warmth of him and this kiss that I never want to end.

But of course it has to. I pull away first, not wanting him to be the one to break away.

He smiles. "Wow."

"You can say that again."

He nuzzles my neck, his lips settling against my ear. "Wow," he murmurs.

I blink in an effort to clear the haze that's muddled my brain. No one can see us here, but surely someone saw us duck behind the bushes and god only knows what they think we're up to. I blush, knowing they'd be right.

"Do you still want to see the animals?"

"Besides you?" I smile up at him, and my heart nearly thuds out of my chest at the softness in his eyes. How could I have not seen this—or even thought about this—before?

He laughs, a deep rumble that sends chills down my spine, and pulls me closer.

Lord help me.

His mouth covers mine and I melt into him. Our tongues dance lightly, softly, like we have all the time in the world and this is the most important thing we have to do.

This time he pulls away. He presses his lips to my temple, the one that always hurts first when I get a headache, then stands. Taking my hand, he tugs me to him and folds me into his embrace.

I could get used to this.

"Come on." We walk to the main path, and I glance at the fence where we entered to make sure no one's watching for us. They don't seem to be. The elderly couple hasn't moved. A man sits by himself beneath a shady tree, and different families surround the fountain. At least I think they're different families—the strollers and toys and frazzled mothers all kind of look the same.

Sunlight filters through the trees, casting long shadows over the path. I'm grateful we're walking. I usually have to close my eyes at this time of day and it's nice to be able to actually enjoy the late afternoon sun. Especially the way it catches the highlights in Cam's dark hair.

I wish I'd brought my camera.

He gives me a sidelong glance and squeezes my hand. "What'cha thinking?"

"I was just wondering why the hell it took us so long to do that."

He lifts my hand to kiss it and butterflies zip through me. "I thought the same thing."

I look up at him. "And?"

He turns us down a path leading to a two-story building with an atrium. "I guess I was afraid we'd ruin our friendship. But I gotta tell you, right now that seems like a stupid reason."

I stop so suddenly that Cameron, still holding my hand, jerks around.

"What's wrong?"

I look up at the building, a slight tremor running through me.

It's the monkey house.

"I don't want to go in there."

"To the monkey house? You're serious?"

I narrow my gaze at him and refuse to budge.

"Okay, you're serious. But what do you have against monkeys? You've never said anything about them before."

I take a step back. "It's not the monkeys. It's the building. My dad..." I turn around and hurry towards a bench. I need to sit down.

Cameron runs to catch up, puzzlement darkening his features. "How do I not know that you have a thing with the monkey house?"

I snort. "I don't have a thing, I just can't go in there." Dad's seizure last night blurs with memories of the one all those years ago, and I can't catch my breath. I sink onto the bench and reach for Cameron's hand, tugging him next to me. "One of my earliest memories is my dad having a seizure. In there." I nod at the building and the atrium winks back at me. I blink against the reflection.

"I don't get it. He has them a lot." He tilts his head, trying to understand the craziness that is my brain. "You still go in your house."

"I know, but this was the first one that I remember. All the others…" how do I explain this? "It's like I compare every other one to the first one. It was so awful—the monkeys screaming and my mom crying over my dad while everyone stared—that I've never been able to forget it. I guess I'm afraid that going inside would make the memories even stronger."

The darkness in his face shifts. "That I get."

His sister, duh. I'm whining about a scary memory and his sister is gone. Presumed dead. And he was a suspect. "Yeah, I guess you do." I rub my thumb over his fingers. "So can we skip the monkeys?"

He pulls me close, wrapping his arm around my shoulders. "We'll go wherever you want."

I lean my head against his shoulder, thinking. A slow smile spreads across my face. "The bat house."

He jerks away. "Bats?" He looks at my beaming face and shakes his head. "Just when I think I understand you."

But it makes perfect sense. They live in complete darkness; the triggers for my headaches and everything else are non-existent in their world. If it wasn't for the poop I'd contemplate actually living in a bat house. That, and the fact that bats freak the shit out of me.

◆ ◆ ◆

Cameron drapes his arm over my shoulders as we leave the bat house. "I knew you were messing with me."

It turns out it wasn't as cool as I expected. Yes, it was dark, but bats are noisier than I thought and bear an alarming resemblance to rats. Flying rats that screech and swoop and stink. A lot.

The sun has sunk lower in the sky, lengthening the shadows until they completely cover the grounds. Animals pace near the rear of their open-air cages, waiting for their dinner. People huddle near the guardrails, anxious for a glimpse of the carnage.

My stomach growls. "So what's next? More breaking and entering? Maybe knocking over a taco stand?"

"You hungry?"

I nod against his shoulder and we turn awkwardly towards the rear of the zoo. Our bodies aren't familiar enough with each other to walk arm and arm with the same gait. I trip when our hips collide, then he steps on my toe. I pull away and slide my fingers through his.

There's no sign of whoever chased us near the back fence, but we wait a few minutes before slipping through the creaky gate.

Inside the car I crank the heater and sit on my hands. As much as I bitch about the sunlight, at least it keeps me warm.

Cameron drives to McDonald's and he places our usual

order—two quarter pounders, two large fries, two orange sodas—then parks so we can eat.

I rip open the paper and take a huge bite, but I'm unable to swallow. Stupid butterflies just reminded me that I'm inhaling my hunk of meat in front of the boy I like. I've never been one of those girls who can't eat in front of guys, but I do try to use a little self-control. I peek at Cameron through my hair and laugh.

He's halfway through his burger and has a handful of fries at the ready. He must sense me watching because he juts his chin at my food. "I thought you were hungry."

I still have a lump of burger in my mouth, so I just nod and chew slowly.

We eat quietly—well, as quietly as one can eat with a seventeen-year old boy—then he starts the car. "Is the boat ramp cool?"

"Yeah, sure." My heartbeat quickens. It won't be the same with other people, but I'm kind of excited to see what people will say when they realize me and Cameron are… together.

Chapter 11

A half-dozen kids are sitting on the trunks of their parked cars when we arrive. Some alternative band I don't recognize is blaring from an mp3 player. It's too early for a fire and the chill from the river goes straight through my sweater.

"Do you still have that blanket?"

Cameron retrieves it from the trunk and we glance nervously at each other before approaching our friends. I texted Amelia after we ate so I knew she'd be here in a little while, but I wished she'd hurry up. Now that heads were turning our way I wish we'd gone someplace else. I'm not ready for this—

"New couple alert!" Our friend Joey props an elbow against

his windshield and eyes us. "When did this happen?"

"No wonder you two've been MIA," said Jason, Joey's partner-in-crime. I've known Joey and Jason, or Double J as we all call them, almost as long as I've known Cameron. With their light brown shaggy hair and blue eyes they could almost pass for twins, and I suspect they've encouraged that impression.

Cameron presses his hand against the small of my back, lifting the hem of my sweater until his fingers brush my skin. A jolt of electricity shoots through my stomach and keeps heading south. Heat flushes my face and it suddenly occurs to me that everyone is staring.

"So?" asks Travis, a scrawny guy who tags along with Double J. He's supposedly a kick-ass wrestler, but I find him obnoxious. He's always trying too hard. "You two gonna talk or you want us to guess?" He elbows Jason. "I bet I can come up with a good story."

"Travis, quit being a jackass."

I smile at Haley, Travis's girlfriend. I can't for the life of me figure out why she wastes her time with him. They spend most of their time either fighting or ignoring each other, but hey, who am I to criticize?

Cameron laughs. "It's no big deal. I finally convinced Biz she's been wasting her time with those putzes and—"

No one speaks.

I turn around and my heart sinks. Robbie is standing behind us. He must have gone to the woods to pee. "Thanks for the warning, assholes," I mutter.

"Putz?" Robbie answers Cameron but he's glaring at me. "It's bad enough you already found some other guy to follow you around, but you gotta talk shit about me, too?"

"Cam is not some guy."

Cameron opens his hand so his entire palm is flattened against my back. Distracting me. "Biz, save your breath. He's not worth it."

"That's not what she thought two weeks ago."

"Dude, let it go. No one else gives a shit."

"I can't believe you're even wasting your time with her. You know she'll drop you in a couple weeks, just when you start to really like her."

Those last words sting. I never meant to hurt Robbie but that's exactly what I've done. And now we're rubbing his face in it. "Cam, let's just go."

Robbie flexes his fists, his body tense. "Don't do me any favors." He scans our friends' faces. "I'm outta here." He jams his hand in his pocket and yanks out his keys, then storms across the parking lot to his car. "Figures she's sticking by him now that another kid is missing."

Cameron's grip on my hand tightens and my jaw drops. No one says a word.

Did he really just say that? Do people think still Cameron had something—

A spray of gravel cuts off my thoughts.

"Very mature!" I shout after him.

Joey slaps his hand on the trunk of his car. "Well that was fun. Now who's ready for a drink?"

A beer can sails through the air. Cameron catches it before it smacks me in the chest. Another follows and I flinch. He silently hands one to me, the casual smile from earlier replaced with a scowl.

"Don't pay attention to Robbie," Haley says, smiling at me. "He was bitching about you before you got here. He'll get over it."

Her words don't exactly make me feel better, but I didn't

come here to worry about my ex. Determined to push him out of my head, I open my beer, spraying foam all over my hands. At least it didn't get on my sweater. My parents don't drink and I swear they can smell it even after I've washed my clothes.

Double J and Travis chug half their beers in one gulp, but Cameron takes it easy. We both like to drink with our friends but I get headaches enough without giving myself a hangover. I never really questioned Cameron's reasons, but I'm glad he doesn't like to get trashed.

"Let's sit down." I don't know how Cameron brushes off comments like Robbie's, but I guess he's had years to get used to it. He hands me his beer and I step back so he can spread out the blanket. We settle next to each other and I immediately jump up.

Everyone stares at me.

I lift the edge of the blanket and kick at the gravel. "Got a stone up my ass."

They all laugh and I sit back down, happy to have lightened the mood.

Travis belches. "You know who else's got a stone up his ass?" He launches into a story about the wrestling coach and

I lean back on my hands. Cameron shifts so his arm is against mine and I tune out Travis's yammering. The beer is starting to take effect and I close my eyes, letting the lightheaded-ness take over. This is why I drink. Not to get drunk or feel zuninhibited—that's Amelia's main reason—but to be free of the constant need to keep my flickering in check. Sitting in the darkness, I don't have to worry about flickering accidentally, but it's never far from my thoughts. With beer—I take another sip—all that goes away.

Cameron's head touches mine. "It's nice to see you finally relax."

I smile at him and my breath catches. He's so close, his eyes just inches from mine. The alcohol urges me closer to him but I resist. I'm not into PDA.

But he, apparently, doesn't mind, because in the next heartbeat his lips are on mine and my beer tips on its side.

"Get a room!"

I'd love to.

Wait, that wasn't Haley. I turn around in time to see Amelia a split second before she tackles me. She lands between me and Cameron, spilling whatever was left of my beer all over my jeans.

I wipe my hands down my legs and laugh. Can't do anything about it now. I look around and don't see her car. "How did you—oh." Trace is standing off to the side, shifting from one foot to the other.

Amelia scrambles to her feet and grabs Trace's elbow. "Everyone, you know Trace." Few people at school don't know who he is. The guys all grunt at him. "Trace, this is everyone. And this," she points at me, "is Biz."

We nod at each other and I give her my best what-the-fuck look.

Two beer cans fly through the darkness and land at Amelia's feet. "Thanks, assholes." She picks one up and taps the top. "Trace and I ran into each other shopping for running shoes."

I hold in a smirk. Amelia doesn't run.

She lifts an eyebrow at me. "Anyway, I told him about how you want to interview him for your photo project thing—" Cameron raises an eyebrow at me, "—and we got to talking and I invited him to come along."

Joey cracks open another beer and throws an unopened can at me. This time I catch it. "Pull up a chair. We're just getting started."

I get on my knees and straighten the blanket so they can

sit down. Firm hands wrap around my waist and in one swift motion I'm nestled between Cameron's legs. That works.

Amelia lands cross-legged next to me and Trace sits on the edge of the blanket. He's too far away for Amelia's liking, but after another beer she'll coax him closer.

Jason leans forward, his feet on the bumper. "So Trace, you captain this year?"

He takes a long drink and nods. "Co-captain."

"Can they kick you off the team for drinking?" Joey asks.

Trace holds up his beer and studies the can. "Probably."

Travis raises his can. "Welcome to the club."

Their conversation shifts to sports so I nudge Amelia and eyeball Trace. "Well?" I mouth.

She shrugs and mouths back, "Later."

Cameron's fingers trail down my back and he whispers in my ear. "So what's this about an interview?"

Is he jealous? A flutter kicks in my stomach. I know I'm not supposed to like that in a guy, but coming from Cameron it's really hot. "I was trying to help Amelia. She couldn't get him to notice her so I said I'd offer to take pictures of him and do an interview for our sports page."

He nods at Trace. "You might need to find another idea."

Trace has shifted so his hand is next to Amelia's leg. His thumb rubs the inside of her pant leg where only we can see.

Go Amelia!

The guys burst into laughter and Joey tumbles off the side of the car, landing flat on his back, which makes them laugh even harder.

Boys can be such—

"Dude!" Jason yells. "That's totally what she looks like!"

They all turn to look at me.

"What?"

"You." Joey croaks from the ground. "When you go all spastic in class."

"What?" I repeat. They can't be talking about when I flicker. They can't. No one knows. How could they know?

"You know," Jason laughs, "when you get all twitchy in class, like you just woke up or something."

Fuck! I crack open the second beer and take a long drink. "Yeah, that." I'm trying to play it cool but now they're really staring at me. I take another drink and my head spins.

Amelia giggles next to me. "You guys are ridiculous." Thank

you Amelia. "If she's sleeping how does she know she's twitching?" Okay, not helping so much.

I set the beer down—that's definitely not going to help—but I can't think of anything to say. My mind's gone blank.

"You okay?" Cameron whispers.

Frustration pushes away my embarrassment. I hate people asking me that, but more than that, I hate having him worry about me. "I'm fine. Sorry. I guess I didn't expect to be the butt of the joke."

Everyone relaxes. Joey stands up and brushes himself off. "That's why it's so funny."

By now everyone is getting buzzed so I don't have to wait long before the conversation moves to something else, but my exuberance is gone. I'm beyond happy to have Cameron so close, but my typical worries come crashing back.

Midway through her second beer Amelia nudges me. "I have to pee."

"You can't wait?"

"No. Come with me."

I stand up, my stiff legs groaning in protest.

Cameron slides a hand around the back of my thigh and

I want to sink back into his lap. "Be careful." The serious expression on his face sobers me up. I'd forgotten about the real danger lurking out there.

"We will."

Amelia loops her arm through mine and scans the group on the cars. "Haley, you need to go?"

"Yes! Wait up." There's rustling of jackets and the clink of a beer can being set on a car as Haley disentangles herself from Travis.

We pick our way around the cars and find the narrow path at the edge of the tree line. The boat ramp doesn't have any outbuildings so the bathroom is the woods. Faint light illuminates the spot where we're parked, but the three feet into the forest and we're blind.

"Do you guys know where we're going?" Haley fumbles for my arm and latches on. "I can't see shit."

I trip over a tree root and nearly take them both down with me.

Amelia bursts out laughing. "I guess this is far enough. Make sure you're uphill. I'm not responsible for which way my piss flows." She unzips and in seconds the quiet is replaced with the sound of her peeing.

Haley and I scramble further down the path, clinging to each other. I sure as hell am not getting pissed on. I stop next to a hollowed out tree while Haley inches further down the path. A car engine revs in the distance, and headlights shine through the trees.

The ridiculously straight trees.

I never noticed how evenly spaced they are.

The headlights get brighter and my fingers twitch.

No. I close my eyes but it's too late.

"Haley. Amelia. Hurry up."

"I'm almost done." Plants rustle as Haley tries to keep her balance. Moments later I hear her zipper, then she's standing next to me, once again clinging to my arm.

But the tingling has already started.

The car drives alongside the tree line, lighting us up as if we had a spotlight on us. I know I can't flicker this way, but I can't stop the heaviness that crashes onto me. I fight to stay on my feet.

Haley stumbles beneath my sudden weight. "Biz, what are you doing?"

"What's going on?" Amelia's at my side.

"She just collapsed."

"Biz, how much did you drink?"

I can't answer them. I can't move. They're staring at me like I've grown a third head and I wish I could explain that I'll be weightless in a second and then we can walk back to our friends like nothing happened. But right now I can't make my body respond.

And like that the heaviness lifts and I'm back on my feet. "Sorry. That beer really hit me." I slip an arm through each of theirs and take a step towards the parking lot.

"Are you sure you're okay?" Haley asks. "You practically passed out."

Amelia squeezes my arm. "She's fine. Nothing another beer won't fix, right Biz?" She knows I don't drink much and while I'm grateful she doesn't say anything more in front of Haley, I know she's going to want an explanation.

I force a laugh. "Exactly."

We burst out of the woods, all laughter and squeals. Haley doesn't realize we're faking, which means most of the guys won't either. Cameron will know something's wrong the second I sit down. That's just how he is.

The three of us split off towards our guys. I squat near Cameron. "I'm ready to go."

"What the hell took you so long?" Kirk asks.

"Yeah," Joey laughs. "We were about to send out a search party. We thought maybe you'd gotten kidnapped."

While everyone laughs, Cameron stiffens next to me.

Yes, it's definitely time to go.

"Joey!" Amelia yells as Jason punches him in the arm.

"What?"

"Cam," Haley whispers loud enough that we all hear.

Cameron's breathing's grown shallow. He's working his jaw, clenching and unclenching like he's ready to tear Joey a new one.

Joey's mouth drops open, late to the clue bus once again. "Dude, sorry. I wasn't thinking about—"

"Just drop it."

"Shit, man."

The uncomfortable silence amplifies every sound from the forest. Crickets chirping, weird hoots, and a freakishly loud branch snapping.

Suddenly Haley laughs much louder than necessary. "You guys, Biz totally passed out when Amelia was peeing!"

Cameron's head whips towards me, along with everyone else's. "You did?"

"Just for a second. It's no big deal." I search out his eyes in the darkness. The guys snicker. "Can we please just go?"

"Yeah." He pulls me to my feet. "You guys can hang on to the blanket, just make sure I get it back at school."

Trace holds out his hand and they do one of those guy hand-shakes that only makes sense to them. "Sure thing. Thanks."

Amelia looks up at me, uncertainty and excitement battling on her face. "Call me later."

"I will." My hand lifts in a half-hearted wave. "Bye guys. See you Monday."

"Good luck, Cam," Travis calls out. "Looks like you're gonna need it."

Chapter 12

"What an ass." I stomp towards Cameron's car, not caring if Travis can hear me. "He always has to say something to ruin my night."

Cameron unlocks the car but doesn't open the door. Instead he wraps his arms around me and pulls me close against his chest. "I wouldn't say it's ruined."

My body responds and I relax into him. "Okay, maybe ruined is too strong."

"In fact, except for a couple dumbass comments, I think this has been a pretty good night."

Our kiss at the zoo plays through my mind. "You have a point." I stand on my tiptoes and brush my lips against his throat.

He sighs softly, his breath warm on my face. "See, Travis doesn't know what he's talking about. I'm already lucky."

My shoulders tense and I pull back. "Getting a little ahead of yourself, aren't you?"

He jerks his head, confused for a moment before he realizes what I mean. "No! God, Biz, I didn't mean that." His hands slide into my hair and he cradles my head. He brushes the tip of his nose against mine. "I meant I'm already lucky because you're here with me."

If I wasn't close to melting earlier, I am now. "Oh."

Our lips meet and I pull him closer. He traces my jaw with his thumb, sliding it lower down my throat, making my pulse stutter. The kiss deepens. The taste of him fills my head and I grip the back of his shirt like it's the only thing keeping us connected.

He breaks off the kiss but his lips don't stop. His mouth travels to where his thumb had been and settles at the curve of my collarbone. The heat from his tongue sends chills down my back and a tingling sensation races through me, but without the fear I have when flickering. There's nothing scary about this.

He lifts his head and nuzzles my other ear. "We should get

out of here."

I can't get in the car fast enough.

Cam drives slowly, taking extra care when turning onto the main road. He only had one beer, but we are a few years shy of legal drinking age.

Cameron's hand settles on my knee. "Where to?"

"I should probably go home." I'd love to spend the rest of the night with him, but I'm worried about Dad. My being there doesn't really do anything for him, but Mom could use the moral support. Or the help in case he has another seizure.

He moves his hand so he's gripping the inside of my knee and winks. "You sure?"

My heart races. I smile. "No. But I am worried about my dad."

His smile falls. "Right."

We ride through town in silence. I keep replaying the kiss at the zoo—the feel of Cameron's lips on mine, how safe I felt in his arms—and can't believe he's sitting right next to me. My gaze drops to his hand still caressing my leg. This all feels like a dream.

"So what happened in the woods?"

Cameron's voice startles me out of my daydream. "Oh, you know Haley. She's drunk and made a big deal that I tripped."

"It didn't sound like you tripped."

"Well I did have a couple beers."

He nods, lips tight.

"What?"

"You don't want to hear it."

"Just say it."

He rubs his hand over my thigh. "I'm worried about you."

"Oh." It's not that I don't want to hear that—of course I like that he's concerned about me—but I don't like him worrying. "What can I say to change that?"

His voice is quiet. "I don't know."

He doesn't speak again until he parks around the corner from my house. He kills the engine and shifts so he's facing me, then lifts his hand to my face. "Whatever's going on," he looks down, then back into my eyes, "you know you can trust me."

"I do trust you."

His fingers weave through my hair, settling just behind my ear. "Then tell me what's going on with you." He closes his eyes. "You already know all my secrets."

I touch my fingertips to his eyelids and he turns his face to kiss my palm. An unfamiliar emotion fills my heart, my throat, and finds its way to my head, where it leaks out of one eye. I quickly brush away the tear before he notices.

His eyelids flutter open. His dark eyes gaze into mine and whatever I planned to say is lost. I lean closer and his lips meet mine. We cling to each other with a ferocity I've never felt before. As the kiss grows more urgent, all sense of self-control slips away and I melt into his arms.

My phone beeps, breaking the mood. "Crap," I mumble into Cameron's mouth. "I've got ten minutes to get home." Amelia came up with the idea after the third time I got grounded for missing curfew.

He starts the engine and putters around the corner, stopping in front of my house. The only light on my street comes from the streetlight on the corner and the porch light over my front door. Old Berta grinds to a halt in front of my house.

The dashboard clock reads 11:52. "Just in time."

"So, uh…" he clears his throat. "I had a really good time tonight. It's different with you since we already know each other, you know? It's kinda nice not worrying so much."

"What do you mean so much?" Relax. I take a deep breath. "I mean, what are you worried about?"

He shrugs. "Just what I said before. About ruining our friendship."

"Cameron, I can't tell you when I've ever felt like this about anyone. Part of me still can't believe this is happening, but I'm really happy it is. It feels right, you know?"

He rests his hand on my knee. "I do."

My hand moves to the door handle, but Cameron reaches over me and opens it for me. "Let me get that for—"

I lay a kiss on him before he can finish his sentence. Technically, I'm home.

His fingers twine through my hair, pulling me close, while his other hand fumbles with my seatbelt. The latch clicks and I try to climb over the seat but my leg catches on the shifter. He slides a hand beneath me and lifts me onto his lap so my feet are on the passenger seat, but rather than kissing me, he tucks my head against his chest and holds me.

I want to stay here forever. I can deal with being grounded. Just let this moment last a little longer.

After a few minutes he lifts my chin with his finger so he's looking in my eyes. He brushes a soft kiss on my lips. "I don't want you to get in trouble."

I sigh. "Thank you for tonight. I had a really good time, too." So good, in fact, that I've already made up my mind to relive tonight. I kiss him one last time then climb back to my seat and open the door. "I'll talk to you tomorrow."

I'll also see you yesterday, but I won't be changing a thing.

Chapter 13

I wake up before dawn to study for my trig test. The last time I flickered on back-to-back days I ended up in the hospital, and since I'm determined to repeat last night, I better ace this test on my own.

But really? Trig? Who decided this was important information for adulthood? After half an hour I toss the book to the floor and grab my phone. I start to text Amelia, then remember it's still dark out. She'd kick my ass if I woke her up, especially after a night of drinking.

Maybe food will help.

I trudge downstairs and find Dad sitting at the kitchen table.

"You got in late." He doesn't exactly frown, but the wrinkles around his eyes are deeper than normal. He studies me over the rim of his coffee cup as he takes a sip.

"How are you feeling? Can I get you anything?"

"Don't change the subject." He sets down his cup. "I know you don't like to hear it, but I worry about you Biz." He shakes his head as I open my mouth to protest. "With your headaches… you need to take better care of yourself. Staying up late and drinking—"

How does he know I was drinking?

"—are only going to make your symptoms worse."

"I wasn't—"

He cuts me off with a look. "You forget who you're talking to. I wish you'd trust me. Drinking is only going to make it worse." The clock ticking over the stove suddenly sounds like a hammer drilling into my skull. Dad's normally watery eyes are clear, focused, and boring into mine. Like he's trying to tell me something without actually telling me.

I blink and my gaze drops to the floor.

"I don't mean to pry, I'm just—"

I look up. "Worried about me. I know. Can't we talk about something else?"

He smiles. "How's Robbie?"

Ugh, wrong topic. "We broke up last week."

His face falls. "You seem to be taking it okay…"

"Yeah, well…" I bite my lip. Telling him about Cameron will make it more real than it already is. It's not like he can take away what's happened, but telling your parents makes it… official.

He watches me, his lips twitching. There's that damn patience again.

But this time I'm not biting. It's too soon.

"How's school?"

I shrug, and he lets out an exasperated sigh.

"Biz, I'm trying here. I want to know what's going on in your life. I feel like…" he shakes his head. "I don't know. I guess sometimes I'm afraid that if I don't make the effort now it'll be too late and then I'll have missed my chance."

My heart clenches. Why do I fight his efforts to be a good dad? I have friends who'd kill for this kind of attention from their parents. I lean forward and place my hand on his. "Dad, you haven't missed anything. I just don't have anything interesting going on in my life." Besides flickering and making out with Cameron and strange men knowing too much about me.

His eyes narrow slightly and I shrink away. "Do you ever..." he stops. His head dips and he rubs the stubble on his chin with his thumb and forefinger.

That's okay. I can play the patience game, too.

He tries again. "With your headaches, how do you feel? I mean, I understand that there's pain and light makes it worse, but does anything else happen?" He's looking at his hands so doesn't see the look of pure panic that's frozen on my face.

I clear my throat. "Like what?"

"I don't know." He flexes his fingers. I can't tear my eyes away from them. "Any other side effects?" He continues stretching, pushing his arms above his head and rolling his shoulders.

Exactly like I do when I'm fighting the weight that crushes me just before I flicker.

"You mean like an aura?" I'd read that some people who get migraines have visual disturbances that distort how they see things.

"That's one thing." He straightens his fingers, then lays his palms flat on the table. It's like he wants to tell me something, but either can't or doesn't know how.

Either way, he's got me completely freaked out.

He takes a quick breath. "Do you ever have..." his fingers

twitch, "a weird feeling in your hands or feet?"

I look up from his fingers to find him looking me in the eye, gauging my reaction. I snap my mouth closed.

He can't know.

He continues. "Because if you do, you can tell me." The corners of his eyes sag, followed by a frown that makes him look sad, desperate.

For a second I consider telling him everything. The lights, the tingling, the flickering. I long to have someone on my side, someone I can share this… condition… with, to not have to endure this by myself. But despite what he says, I don't know how he could understand.

My gaze flits all over the room. He'll break my resolve if I let him stare at me much longer. As much as I hate to, I push back my chair and stand up. "Thanks Dad. But really, there's nothing to tell." I turn away, but not before his face falls. I straighten my shoulders and try to push the guilt away, but it clings to my chest, crushing my lungs.

Once I'm out of view, I bend at the waist and force a breath. I need to focus right now.

I return to my room and flip open my trig book. Surely

if I stare at it long enough the funny little words will start to make sense. They have to because—I check the clock on my nightstand—I'm leaving in an hour to flicker.

Fifty-eight minutes later I shrug into my jacket and leap down the stairs two at a time, nearly colliding with Mom. "Whoa, sorry. I'm just going for a drive." I peek in the living room. "Where's Dad? He was up earlier."

She touches the side of her face, much the same way I do when I have a migraine. I wonder if I picked that up from her, or if she even realizes she does it. "He went back to bed. Said he wasn't feeling well."

My shoulders slump. The ache in my chest hadn't exactly left, but now it's back in full force. "Is it serious? Does he need to go back to the hospital?" I know that's not it but I can't not ask.

"It's probably just a reaction to all the drugs they gave him. He should be back to normal by tomorrow."

Normal for Dad isn't what I'd wish on anyone, but it's the best we can hope for.

"Please be home in time for dinner."

"I will." I brush my cheek against hers and step into the blinding sunlight.

◆ ◆ ◆

I'm gonna miss the zoo.

Cam had picked me up at four and I wanted to repeat every second of our date, but it's already noon. When I flicker I go back eighteen hours. I've stopped trying to figure out the significance of that number—the best I can come up with is it has something to do with my age. I'm seventeen years and eight months, which is pretty damn close to eighteen. If the time frame shifts it's too subtle for me to tell.

At least this way I'll get to eat again. I'm starving.

The car practically drives itself, turning at the end of my street and following the curve of the river. A niggle of worry works its way into my belly, but I push it aside. Yes, it's noon. Yes, the sun is practically at its highest point in the sky. But that's why the Strand is the Strand.

The trees soar high over the road, arching ever so slightly at the top. Something to do with the path of the sun and them angling to absorb the most nutrients.

Yeah, I actually paid attention in biology.

The arch is important because it means the light still passes through the trees even though it normally wouldn't in a regular row of trees. I have to drive on the east side of the road for it to work, but fortunately that's the direction I'm already heading. Yes, I liked geology, too. Anything having to do with people and our physical surroundings. Math and English, not so much.

I round the next bend in the road and the Strand winks at me. A breeze stirs the leaves near the highest point, but that won't affect me. I'm more concerned with what's holding them up.

Two seconds later my fingers twitch. The tingling numbness sweeps through my hands and I fight to keep my foot steady on the gas. My eyelids flutter but remain open. Martinez's comment about my pupil dilating flashes through my mind, but it's gone just as fast because I'm sinking into my seat. My arms fight to let go of the steering wheel but I will them to hang on. I can barely see over the top of the dashboard. My head's so heavy…

Then it lifts and I'm nearly hitting the roof of the car. Almost…

I cling to the steering wheel, fighting for breath as my eyes roll back and—

I'm choking on a fry. There's already a drink in my hand so I take a big sip and cough again.

Cameron drops his burger into his lap and reaches over to pat my back. Concern darkens his eyes and I nearly forget the food lodged in my throat. "Are you okay?"

I take another sip. "Yeah," I croak. "I'm fine."

He smiles and his hair falls over his eyes.

Better than fine.

Chapter 14

Flickering has its consequences. Most notably a pounding, piercing, vomit-worthy explosion that happens when I get back to the point before I flickered. It's Sunday morning and I'm on my bed studying when the pain hits me out of nowhere. I usually check what time I leave so I can at least be ready for it, but that doesn't lessen the severity.

I push my book to the floor and bury my face in the pillow. It was worth it, it was worth it, it was so totally worth it. It sucks now but I chose to flicker and I have to deal with it. Besides, who else gets to relive a night like that?

My phone beeps.

I can't.

It beeps again.

And again.

I drag myself out of bed and grab my phone off the floor. It's Amelia and she just acronym-ed all over my phone. I choose to call her instead of texting so I don't have to open my eyes. "So it went well?"

"Ohmigod! He's so effing hot! Did you see him last night?"

I pull the phone away from my ear. "Yes, I saw how hot he was." Both times. It's weird how no one else deviates from what they did the first time. Only me. "So what happened after we left?"

She sighs dramatically. "We hung out for awhile and he put his arm around me. Thank you so much for leaving the blanket! I told him I was cold so he pulled it around us…" she trails off and I'm grateful for the quiet. I really am happy for her, I just wish she wasn't so loud about it.

"Did you kiss?"

"Yeah, when he drove me home. Holy crap he's hot. And you still totally have to do the interview. He's really excited about it and of course I'm going to his games."

I smile. "That's awesome, Amelia. We'll definitely go Tuesday." I'm happy she's so excited and it's fun to be feeling this at the same time as her.

"So what about you? I saw you guys making out before you left. Did anything else happen?"

I think back to last night. I had debated changing things but it was already perfect. I can't imagine wanting anything different. "He just drove me home."

"And...?"

"Not much. But it was awesome." I've shared more with her about other guys, but I want to keep Cameron to myself.

◆ ◆ ◆

I spend the rest of the day in my room, alternating between sleeping and trying to study. Mom calls me down for dinner, but I can't eat. I force down a couple bites of apple—there's some theory that it helps migraines but I don't know if it actually does anything—then crawl back into bed.

There's a text from Cameron waiting for me. "Thinking of you." I'd hug the phone if it wasn't so damn small and completely unhuggable.

"Me too. Going to sleep soon."

"Wish I was there."

I'm melting. I'm literally melting into my bed right now. "Good night."

I plug in my phone and flip off the light. I'm not letting trig destroy my good mood.

◆ ◆ ◆

Morning comes too soon. The ice pick in my ear has been replaced with a knitting needle—the pain is just as severe but in a more specific place—and it feels like half my brain leaked out overnight. I roll out of bed in search of another apple and coffee. And my meds.

I fumble in the dark in the medicine cabinet. Bottles of lotion and hair stuff fall all around me, landing on my feet. "Shit!" I jump and hit my head in the open cabinet. "Are you kidding me?" I say to no one.

Or I thought no one. Mom is standing in the doorway, the light from the hall casting her face in shadow. "I wasn't sure if you'd go to school today. How are you feeling?"

I shrug. Same old, same old.

"Are you sure you don't want to stay home?" She moves closer and places her cool hand on the back of my neck.

I purr against her. "Can't. Trig test."

"You can't make it up?"

I can't even explain how grateful I am to have understanding parents. Someone seriously needs to punch me the next time I'm bitching about them worrying too much. But they aren't understanding about failing grades. "I'm already cutting it a little close in that class. I don't think I can miss today."

Her fingers knead my neck, working on a knot wedged just beneath the base of my skull.

"That feels good."

She places her other hand on the side of my face and presses a kiss to my forehead. "Just don't overdo it. I'd rather you have to take this class over than end up in the hospital."

I shudder.

With one last squeeze, she releases me and steps into the hall. "Black coffee?"

I nod weakly. "Yes, please." I scrounge through the jumble of bottles on the floor and come up with my beacon of hope.

The directions read "One as needed" but I'm tempted to take two. If I need one now, then another in five minutes, who's to say I'm not following the directions? I place one on my tongue, but hesitate. My doctor's gone on and on about overdosing and the increased risk of bleeding to death if I accidentally walk into a wall or some other inanimate object. Which isn't unheard of given the fact that my meds make me a little loopy.

Taking a deep breath, I put the second pill back in the bottle. I do want to be able to concentrate for this test, otherwise what's the point of dragging my ass out of bed?

Still in the dark, I pull my hair into a loose ponytail, then go back to my room to throw on some clothes. My trig book laughs at me and I kick it across the floor. Bastard. I sigh and fish it out from under my bed. I can probably study a little more before class.

Downstairs Mom's already poured coffee into a travel mug. An apple and an apple-flavored granola bar sit on the counter next to my car keys, along with a sticky note that reads 'Good luck'. I shove everything into my backpack and head out the front door.

Chapter 15

"How'd you do?" Amelia heaves her book into her locker and slams it shut.

"Better than I expected. I studied my ass off yesterday but I think I'm lucky if I got a B."

She leans the back of her head against the bank of lockers, her eyes closed. "I totally bombed it. Trace and I were texting all day and I couldn't concentrate."

Regret courses through me. If I hadn't flickered on Sunday I could still repeat today, then I could help Amelia. She doesn't know how I sometimes know exactly what will be on the tests, and she doesn't ask. Once last year she dropped hints about an older student selling answers, but I didn't bite and she hasn't asked again.

She opens one eye. "Have you talked to Cam?"

"A little." I smile, and I hope it's not the same dreamy one that's plastered on Amelia's face. I'm all smooshy inside but that doesn't mean I want everyone else knowing that. "I have a migraine so I slept most of the day."

"I didn't want to say, but you do look a little... awful."

I swat her shoulder, then wince at the movement. "Thanks."

She blows me an air-kiss and turns to walk down the hall to her next class. "Anytime, babe."

I head the opposite way and a hand slides around my waist.

Cameron nuzzles my neck as we walk, one hand planted firmly on my lower back. "I wasn't sure if you'd be here today."

"I'd rather not be." I smile up at him. "But my day just got considerably better."

He chuckles, a low sound from deep in his chest, and my insides stir. For a second I forget about the pain and nausea and I feel surprisingly lucid. I don't realize I've stopped walking until Cameron pulls at my arm. "We're gonna be late."

"Right." I don't know what just happened, but I want more of it.

By the next day I'm feeling almost back to normal. Good

thing, because the soccer game is today and I have to be Ms. Sports Photographer and run all over the place taking pictures.

I'm waiting at my car for Amelia. The last bell rang ten minutes ago but she still hasn't shown.

My phone buzzes. "Coming!"

Two minutes later she bursts from the side entrance, her face flushed. The red deepens when she sees me. "Sorry!"

I laugh. How can I be mad when she's so happy? I open my door. "Let's go."

She pouts at me from over the hood. "Are you sure you don't want to watch them warm up? Trace has a new formation he's trying and—"

I roll my eyes. "I need food. Trace will still be here in twenty minutes."

With a dramatic sigh she climbs in the car and starts texting.

At this rate I may not need to interview him after all, although it's an easy way to fill in the story part of the project. "I refuse to ask him questions if you're hanging all over each other."

"Me?" She flattens her hand against her chest. "I don't hang, I support. I—" she bursts out laughing. "Okay fine, I'll give you five minutes."

Half an hour later we're camped on the bleachers, surrounded by thirty or so students and about as many parents. The game hasn't started yet and I hope for the guys' sake that more people show up. Having never been to a game myself, I don't know how many people usually attend soccer games, but I figured there was a fan club or something.

Trace runs onto the field, followed by the rest of the team.

Amelia's on her feet. "Go, Trace!"

"He hasn't done anything yet."

"Legs that hot deserve screaming."

She's got me there.

I pull out my equipment and scan the field. The sun is in the west, obviously, so I'll probably move so it's behind me. Although I could get some cool shots with the shadows…

"Do you want me to walk around with you?"

"No, you stay here and scream your little heart out."

She throws a napkin at my head and glances at my uneaten sandwich. "I thought you were starving."

I touch my stomach. "I was." My headache's fading, too. The anticipation of an afternoon taking pictures has completely distracted me. The heft of the camera in my hand draws my focus away from Amelia and back to the field. I'm anxious to start.

When the first whistle blows I step over the seats and walk towards the western corner of the field. The ball sails to the opposite end, so I plop on my butt and get comfortable. They're bound to come this way sooner or later.

A couple of my classmates are on the side opposite the bleachers, cameras glued to their faces. Their shots will all be shit from that angle. I should probably say something, but who am I to tell them what to do? Maybe they're going for a contrasted silhouette.

I watch for Cameron, but he's either out of my line of sight or he's not here. My stomach sinks. Something must have come up. But I don't have time to dwell on it because the whistle blows again and sixteen boys are running straight at me. Two break away from the pack and race after the ball, which is bouncing into the corner.

My corner.

They jostle for position, elbows knocking into ribs, and a guy from the other team sticks his leg out in front of him. I scramble out of the way just as they fall in a tangle on top of my bag.

Whistles and shouts and screams surround me.

"You okay, miss?" The referee holds his whistle inches from his mouth, paused as he waits for my reply. I nod, embarrassed to suddenly have the entire field staring at me. The tripped player picks up the ball and throws it into a cluster of teammates, who jump as one, then fall as one. Miraculously, or so it seems to me, the ball flies over the outstretched hands of the goalie and into the net.

And I'm still sitting on my ass.

The rest of the game is less eventful, although we do score three more times. Trace scored the third—and game-winning—goal and I manage to take a series that, if they turn out as good as I hope, will be my lead story. For the second half of the game I turn my attention to the crowd.

I press zoom and faces fill the display. Toddlers covered in ketchup and ice cream, mothers licking their fingers, ready to spit-bathe their kids. Two girls from my English class sitting close, giggling and pointing at the field. Fathers looking bored, then jumping up every time their child touches the ball, their faces lighting with pride.

Not everyone looks excited to be here. Two or three men

stare at the field as if out of obligation, while another at the end of the bleachers is angled so he's watching the spectators.

And still no Cam.

"Ohmigod, that was so awesome! Biz, did you see Trace's goal? It was so fast no one even came close to stopping it!" Amelia's waiting for me at the bottom of the bleachers. Waiting may not be the right word. More like bouncing.

I wave my camera at her. "I got some kick-ass shots of that goal no one could stop." Her eyes widen and I laugh. "Yes, I'll email them to you. But you can't post them until after I turn in my project."

We head towards the sideline where Trace and several guys are talking to their coach. I meant to prepare a few questions, but between the latest headache and the trig test, I forgot.

Trace waves at us, and I've gotta give the guy credit; he smiles at both of us. Amelia never dates the same type of guy and it's hard to tell who's just trying to get into her pants and who's actually a nice guy.

We wait at the edge of the track until the coach slaps them all on the back and Trace approaches.

"So, uh, what do you need to ask me?" His damp hair is

plastered to his forehead and a streak of dirt runs the length of his neck.

I raise my camera. "Just about the game, how long you've been playing, that type of thing. It shouldn't take long." I move around him so the fading light casts a dramatic shadow on his face. "Do you mind if I start with the pictures while the sun's still out?"

"Yeah, sure." He glances at Amelia, who giggles. His arms hang limp at his sides.

"You know what you need?" I look around and point at a soccer ball wedged beneath the bench. Amelia tosses it to him and his body conforms around it: arm looped lazily against the ball, hip cocked, shoulders relaxed. "Perfect." I fire off a dozen shots before he can blink, then move to the other side.

He wipes the back of his hand across his forehead. "That thing takes pictures fast. My phone takes forever between shots."

I smile, impressed he noticed. "Birthday present. It took a lot of convincing, but I love it."

"Biz is an awesome photographer. I bet these can get published in the real paper."

I throw a look at Amelia. Just because I told her what Turner said doesn't mean I want anyone else knowing.

"Really? You think these might get published?" Trace's smile grows broader.

"I wasn't thinking about that. This project comes first. If Turner likes it, then I can submit them." Those last words are heavy on my tongue. Saying it out loud makes my dream seem a little less like a fantasy. I squat so I can get a different angle, and Trace drops the ball and rests one foot on top of it.

"Oh, babe, that looks so great!"

I ignore Amelia and concentrate on the composition. The sun must've been behind a cloud because with the shift in the breeze his features suddenly seem to glow. Please let these turn out as good as I think they will.

A movement from the other end of the bleachers catches my eye. I adjust the zoom so I can look without being obvious, and my eyes narrow as I snap a picture. "Hey, Trace, is that your dad over there?"

They both turn. The man continues watching us.

"No, my parents don't usually come to games."

"That's weird. I wonder who he's waiting for."

Amelia moves to Trace's side and laughs. "Maybe he's

as impressed with your moves as I am." Trace slips his arm around her waist and the three of us start walking towards the gym.

An unsettled feeling sweeps through me as we near the man. He's sitting on the lowest row, playing with his cell phone. He looks up as we pass by.

"Nice game, Trace."

My stomach lurches but Trace just lifts his hand in thanks.

Chapter 16

I'm still weirded out on the car ride home. He was probably someone's dad, but why was he still sitting there after everyone left?

The thought continues to bother me when I get home, but I push it away. I need to sort out Trace's answers and more importantly, I want to find out what happened to Cameron. "I'm home!" I call on my way up the stairs. The phone's already in my hand. I hit send the second my bag hits my bedroom floor.

Cameron answers on the third ring. His voice is scratchy and he sounds exhausted. "Hey, how was the game?"

I get the impression he's just asking out of obligation, and it stings. "It was fine. I almost got trampled but I think I got some good shots. Plus the interview with Trace." My tone falters, I can't help it. I suck at interviewing.

"I'm sure it went better than that. You don't give yourself enough credit."

"Yeah, well, I'll have to take your word on that." I pause. He's sounding a little more normal and I don't know if bringing up his afternoon will change that. "So... where were you? I thought you were coming to the game?"

There's a rustling over the phone, followed by a thump. "I was planning to, then my mom called and asked me to come home."

I sit up, my nerves singing. "Is everything okay? Did something happen?"

"No. Well, nothing new." He sighs. "There's been more updates about that little girl. The one who was kidnapped. The police don't have any leads so..." he trails off.

My stomach lurches. "Did they call you?"

"They called my dad. Said they were just following up on leads, but they asked him where I was when she disappeared."

"Are you kidding me? How could they think—" I stop. I

know why they think that. Everyone knows. Cameron is the closest thing to a suspect the police ever had, so of course they're going to want to know if he has an alibi.

He lets out a long breath. "At least this time I was at school."

"Shit, Cam. I'm sorry. Why didn't you tell me to shut up when I was going on and on about the game?"

"Because I don't want to think about it. That's all we do here. Think about Katie. And now this other girl." His voice breaks and I can't tell if he's simply talking, or repeating his parents' reminders to not ever forget his sister.

I don't know what to say. Anything will sound trivial. "Can I do anything?"

He sighs, a slow, painful expelling of breath. "No."

We hang up shortly after and I'm left staring at my phone. He says I can't help, but there has to be some way I can do more.

My camera calls to me. I remove the card and slip it into the reader that's always connected to my computer. The photo app comes up and I click the button to download. A little voice scolds me for not deleting the bad ones before downloading them, but I'm too lazy. How else am I supposed to complain that I have so many pictures wasting space on my hard drive?

The soccer game replays on my screen. Trace's goal looks even cooler now that I can see it. When I'm taking pictures it's like my subconscious is aware of the scene and lays out the composition for me, but I don't fully grasp what I've captured until it's full-size on my computer.

The computer scrolls to the final image and I gasp. It's the man from the game. He's staring right at me. My hand flutters to my chest and I force a deep breath. I forgot I'd taken his photo.

I save the album, then head downstairs in search of leftovers and find my parents side by side on the couch watching the news. The kidnapping is the lead story.

"Did they find anything new?" I know the answer since Cameron just told me, but I'm curious if my parents will choose to spin it.

Dad twists his neck to see me. "Hey, sweetie. No they still don't have any clues."

I think of Cameron and try to imagine his house right now. He's probably sitting with his parents, comforting them, the TV silent in the background. To my family this kidnapping takes five minutes of our day, but to his it's a reminder of how terribly wrong your entire world can go in those five minutes.

◆ ◆ ◆

Thursday after class I linger by my locker before heading back to the soccer field. The cross country team runs a course that loops around the school and ends on the track, right where I interviewed Trace. Amelia promised she'd meet me there.

Cameron rounds the corner—books in one hand, camera bag slung over his other shoulder—and my heart lifts. He's the same Cameron I've always known, but it's like a layer's been scraped away. Things I hadn't noticed before are suddenly all I see: the way his biceps strain against the fabric of his shirt, the tilt of his head when someone else is speaking, the curve of his lower lip when he's concentrating. Right now his mouth is decidedly frowning.

I fall into step beside him. "Everything okay?"

He waits a beat before answering. "It's just been a long day." He slips on his jacket, then slides his arm through mine as we walk down the hall. He releases me to open the side door.

A blast of cold air welcomes us and I'm grateful Mom insisted I bring my gloves. I zip my coat as we head for the track and flex my fingers. "This should make taking pictures interesting."

"You need a pair of these." He holds up a pair of gloves with the fingers cut off. Loose threads dangle from where the scissors hacked through the yarn.

Apparently I'm not the only one. Every single person from our class is sitting on the bleachers, and every one of them is either blowing on their hands or sitting on them. "You better hang on to those. Could start a riot."

Several heads turn our way as we find an empty spot on the bleachers, but they keep to themselves.

Cameron leans close. "So what's our game plan? I want to get close to the runners. My guess is most people are gonna stay here, so unless we want the same shots as them, we'll need to move. Plus—"

"The sunlight." I interrupt, and he smiles. I point to the western corner where I camped out for the soccer game. "That's where I took all my shots the other day. The lighting is kick-ass."

He stands. "Then let's go over there."

We pick our way back down the bleachers just as the teams walk out to the track. I lift my camera and snap a couple candids—teammates talking to each other, the coach consoling one girl who looks like she might throw up—then follow Cameron to the corner.

He sets his bag in the grass and sits next to it. I start to lower myself to the ground but he grabs me around the waist and pulls me into his lap. "I've missed you," he whispers in my ear. His strong arms wrap around me. My stomach flips, which makes my heart go all crazy, and I'm embarrassed to find myself completely breathless. I squeeze his bare fingertips and he pulls my hands to his mouth. A gentle kiss on each knuckle makes me flush.

"I wish there was a way I could take pictures with you doing that."

He laughs softly, and his breath sends ripples of excitement through me. He turns his head so my fingers brush his cheek. His eyes drift closed.

Have I mentioned he's beautiful?

I lean forward, but we're interrupted by a shout from midway down the field. "Hey you two! Get a room!"

Amelia bounds towards us and I flinch, ready for the tackle that's coming. For as long as I've known her, she's never passed up the opportunity to—

"Oof!"

Her giggle pierces the relative quiet.

Cameron dodged the brunt of it and lies on his side, laughing. "All these years, you think you'd learn."

I sit up and push Amelia off me. "I guess I keep thinking that maybe this once she won't do it."

Amelia grabs my camera. "So what do you got so far?" She flicks through the display. "Ooh, that girl totally just threw up."

Cameron lifts an eyebrow at me. I shrug.

"Man it's freezing out here. Biz, can I borrow your gloves? You can't use them while you're taking pictures anyway."

I reluctantly hand them over and the chill settles into my skin.

"Thanks." She leans back on her hands. "I can't stay long. My parents weren't too happy with my last trig grade and decided I need some quality time listening to music—I mean, studying—after school. Although they probably have a point. Unless I want to spend my post-high school days at community college, I need to get my grades up."

Again, I feel guilty that I couldn't help her on the last test. I silently promise to flicker for the next one.

As if I summoned it, my fingers start to tingle. I press the tips together.

Cameron looks over his shoulder at the setting sun. "What time exactly does 'after school' start?"

"Eh, in a little while."

The sun is barely peeking through the clouds. And I'm sitting still. There's no way I'm flickering. But the tingling grows stronger. I brace myself for the weight when Cameron rubs his hands together.

"Biz, do you want to use my gloves? It's getting really cold."

Color rushes to my cheeks and I slap my hands over them to hide it. Duh, I'm cold. Not flickering. I'd forgotten that's a normal sensation. "Sure, thanks." I shove my fingers inside the unraveling yarn.

Amelia juts her chin down the field. "Hey, isn't that them?"

Cameron and I scramble to our feet, cameras ready. His breathing slows as his shutter click-click-clicks, and I catch myself watching his hands. He and I are drawn to photography for different reasons: for me it's about capturing the light and its effects on the world around me, but for him it's about preserving a moment in time so he can relive it whenever he wants.

I focus on the runners and I'm moving towards them. Zooming. Squatting low so the angles are sharper, more defined.

"Good call." Cameron's a few feet away. Close enough so he's with me, but respecting my space.

Runners streak by, fists in the air as they cross the finish line. A guy whose locker is near mine falls in a heap next to his coach. Two girls from opposing teams high-five each other.

Click-click-click.

I turn my attention to the spectators. The majority of the people in the first couple rows have cameras glued to their faces. A couple have gloves like Cameron's. I'm definitely gonna have to do that. I zoom in on the front row, ready to document my class documenting the race, when I freeze for real this time.

That man is here again. And he's staring at me.

I take a step back, knocking into Cameron.

"Hey!"

"Sorry."

He lowers his camera. Concern darkens his features. "You're really pale. What happened?"

"Nothing. That man is here again and he just freaked me out."

His head whips towards the bleachers. "What man?"

I tug his arm to make him turn away. "Don't stare. It's just some guy we saw the other night at the soccer game. I'm sure he's someone's dad. I mean, why else would he be coming to high school sporting events? He doesn't even cheer..." my voice trails off and a shudder passes through me. The more things I say out loud the creepier this guy sounds.

Cameron's staring at me, his mouth agape. "Why didn't you say anything? He obviously freaked you out."

"But he didn't do anything. He's just watching the games." And me, apparently.

"Still, it seems weird. Maybe we should tell one of the coaches."

"I don't know, Cam. What if it's just my imagination?"

He looks at the crowd.

"I know we're supposed to report anything weird because of that girl, but I don't want to get him in trouble if he's not doing anything."

"Which one is he?"

I focus in on the spot where I'd just seen the man and a chill runs up my spine. "He's gone."

"Okay, but if you see him again will you promise to tell someone?"

I nod. "I got a picture of him the other night."

He stops and looks at me. "You did?"

"Not intentionally, but yeah." An uneasy feeling settles over me at the memory. I'm sure I'm overreacting—people are always telling me I have an overactive imagination. Maybe they're right. "Anyway, I'm sure it's not a big deal."

When we get back to the parking lot, Cameron leans me against Old Berta and rests his hand on the side of my face. "So are we on for the football game Friday night?"

I wave my hands above my head. "Rah, rah."

He laughs and looks around the deserted parking lot. "I'm sure it won't be all bad. At least there'll be more people to talk to." He brushes his lips over my nose. "Not that I really want to talk to anyone else."

I tilt my head back and he presses his lips lightly against mine. We haven't kissed like we did on Saturday, and I kinda want to drag him into the backseat and, uhh… warm up. "Do you have to go right home?"

He sighs, a long drawn-out sound that tells me his answer.

"Your parents?"

"Yeah. I don't know how long this is gonna go on, but for now I need to be home when I can. Hey," he tilts his head, "why don't you come over Saturday?"

I try to fight the smile that plasters itself to my face, but there's no point. Standing on tip-toe, I wrap my arms around his neck. "I'd love to."

He kisses me again, lingering just long enough to make me forget everything around us, then squeezes me tightly. "I'll see you tomorrow."

I climb into my car and wave as I pull away, my mind already on my computer. As anxious as I am to check out my pictures, I want to do a little research on Cameron's sister first.

He's told me what happened a thousand times, but I've always been afraid to read the stories myself. Letting the police think I was with Cameron when Katie disappeared was an impulse, something neither of us considered a big deal at the time, but now the doubt I've always pushed aside is resurfacing.

The house is dark when I get home. There's a note on the kitchen counter.

"We're stopping for dinner after Dad's appointment. Leftovers are in the fridge."

The note is tucked beneath the new pill bowl, a small white dish that replaced the one that broke. Its lack of personality offends me. At least the Mexico bowl pretended to be festive.

I open the fridge and pull out the leftovers. After popping a plate of what looks to be breaded chicken and mashed potatoes in the microwave, I run upstairs to my computer.

I type Katie's name into the search field. Within seconds, link after link fills my screen and I feel kind of stupid for never looking her up before. I click the first link and I'm thrown back to that horrible night four years ago.

"Police still have no leads in the disappearance of Katie James. The seven-year old was last seen by her brother, Cameron, age thirteen, and a schoolmate, also 13. No witnesses have come forward who may have seen what happened.

It is presumed that she was taken by a person or persons who saw her in the front yard and lured her into their car. A white sedan was seen driving erratically in the neighborhood, but the license plate was not noted."

Katie's class picture runs alongside the article, her dark hair clipped away from her face with a pink plastic barrette that matches her pink sweater. An excruciating sense of sorrow pulls my stomach in fourteen directions. The memories of playing with her at Cameron's house are so vivid… I can still remember the way her hair smelled like strawberries and how she always had a stuffed animal in her hand.

Cameron found one of her favorites at the end of the driveway once he realized she was gone. The red and black ladybug she'd gotten for Christmas the previous year lay discarded in a pile of damp leaves, the only indication she'd been near the street.

That was when he called me.

I click back and Katie's dimples are replaced with more articles that say the same thing. White sedan, no witnesses, no sign of her ever again. Then the accusations against Cameron. A picture of him leaving the police station, his parents shielding them with his arms. The police eventually dropped the case against him due to "lack of evidence", but that just meant they couldn't prove anything, and the kids at school never forgot it.

There were a couple leads the following spring when a human skull was found in the woods on the other side of the state, but it turned out to be a boy that disappeared ten years earlier. I scroll through the rest of the list but there isn't anything new about her case. She's been missing four years and is, as most of the articles say, presumed dead.

My finger hovers over the trackpad on my laptop as a thought whispers through my subconscious. I can't imagine they have anything to do with each other, but I wonder... I type in 'kidnapping' and last week's date. A dozen articles pop up, many with the same foreboding headlines. No Witnesses. Girl Missing. Long Brown Pigtails.

Wait, what?

I click the link.

The similarities to Katie's case are eerie. The little girl was playing down the street from her house with several other kids and no one noticed when she left. She was just gone. Two boys remembered a white four-door car that drove by a couple times but neither noticed the driver; they were more concerned with getting out of the street like they'd been taught.

My senses hum. I can't be the only one who's noticed the similarities. The police probably pulled up Katie's file the second this girl disappeared.

So why are the police bothering Cam?

Chapter 17

"Biz, please see me after class."

My stomach sinks as Bishop places my test facedown on my desk. I try to read the expression on his face but he's already moved on to the girl behind me.

Groans follow in his wake.

The one time I actually try. I thought I did better on this one but I'm terrified to look.

Amelia waves at me from across the room. She hasn't gotten hers back yet and raises her eyebrows at my test.

I turn it over. 91. What?

I look over my shoulder. This can't be right. He must have

given me someone else's test. Although that's clearly my name scrawled across the upper right corner.

91?

I give Amelia a thumbs up just as Bishop slaps her test in front of her. She flips the paper over and her shoulders crumble.

Crap. I know it's not my fault but I feel responsible. If I hadn't been so selfish she might have had a chance.

She catches my eye, then turns away. With a shake of her head the playful mood from moments before evaporates.

Bishop returns to the front of the room and drones on and on about inverse functions, but it's not his lecture that's confusing me. If he knows the test is wrong, why did he give it to me?

When class is finally dismissed, Amelia stops in front of my desk.

"I have to stay."

She glances over her shoulder at Bishop, who's sitting at his desk watching us. "What for?"

"Don't know." I get up and she heads towards the door.

"I guess I'll see you after school."

Bishop watches her go, then steeples his fingers beneath his chin, studying me.

"You wanted to see me?"

"Yes." He drops his hands and leans back in his chair like he has all the time in the world.

I eye the clock.

"Biz, I'm proud of how well you did on this test, but I'm concerned with how sporadic your performance is." He straightens. "Your grades are all over the place, which tells me you're just not applying yourself. Now I know trigonometry isn't the most interesting subject but—"

My eyes glaze over. I can't help it. Is he really spouting the glories of trig? I interrupt him. "So you want me to apply myself?"

"Yes and no. It's frustrating as a teacher to see a student who's clearly smart, but just doesn't care."

"It's not that I don't—"

He holds up a hand. "I know you're smarter than what the majority of your test scores show. I'd like to see this kind of effort continue."

I'm not sure if I'm supposed to feel grateful for being noticed or motivated to try try try, but I feel neither. I just want to get to photo class. "Okay, I'll try."

He smiles, a wide grin that he probably thinks looks benevolent, but comes out looking smarmy.

"I gotta go." I run into the hall just as the bell for the next class rings.

Turner's class is surprisingly boring today. Since we've all taken pictures of at least one game, he's working his way around the room to see what we've got so far. That means while he talks to each student for three minutes the rest of us are stuck reading about contrasting light and dark in a composition.

I already know more than I care to about light, but I've been experimenting with shadows. It's crazy how your perspective to the sun can completely change the mood. It might be a boring soccer game, but add a dramatic length of darkness running alongside the player and you have an entirely different effect.

Okay, so I admit, I'm really into this. One thing I've learned in this class that I didn't realize before is how different the same event looks through different people's eyes. We may see the same thing, but depending on our position relative to the subject and the light relative to the camera, not to mention the photographer's interest in the subject, you could end up with totally different results.

I glance across the room at Cameron. He's reading, his fingers twitching over the edge of the page. I rest my hand in the same place on my book and imagine holding his hand.

I'm lost in a daydream when Turner stops next to my desk. "Don't forget what we talked about last week."

My brow furrows.

"The newspaper." He taps my camera. "You've got some good stuff here and I think you'll be surprised by how much you might like getting your work published."

How do I explain that it's not so much a fear of getting rejected, but a fear of having attention directed at me?

"Just keep it in mind."

That shouldn't be a problem if he's planning to remind me every week.

The bell rings a few minutes later and I wait for Cameron outside the door.

"What time do you want to leave?"

I slip my arm through his. "Leave?"

"For the game."

Panic flutters in my chest. "It's an away game?" I wouldn't have agreed to go if I'd known it involved riding in a car in late afternoon.

"Yeah, but it's only a half hour away. And we can finally spend some time alone."

"That sounds wonderful." Dangerous, but wonderful. Driving anywhere at the end of the day is risky but it's even worse when I'm tired or excited or nervous. I do a mental scan of my body; I appear to be all three. Being near Cameron does that to me.

A grin brightens his face and my anxiety wanes. Really, what am I worried about?

We stop by my car so I can grab my sunglasses and a hat. They aren't a guarantee I won't flicker, but they help.

"You can't find any bigger than that?" Cameron leans against the side of the car while I toss my books in the trunk. He snorts. "It's not even that sunny out."

"What?" I run my fingers over the edge of my oversized specs. "I like them." Especially since they block out most of the light. "You want to stand here all day teasing me?"

He dips his head and gives me a quick kiss. "Maybe."

We cross the parking lot to his car and follow a caravan of cars onto the street. I lean my head against the seat and close my eyes.

"Tired?"

"A little. All this school spirit stuff is exhausting."

"I wonder if there'll be a lot of people at the game."

I peek at him. "It'd be kinda nice if there aren't."

The light turns red and he downshifts, then reaches for my hand and links his fingers through mine.

The touch of his skin anchors me, preventing me from drifting into the discombobulated haze that sometimes envelopes me when I'm riding in a car with my eyes closed. Flashes filter through my sunglasses. I lower the brim of my hat with my free hand.

Cameron squeezes my hand. "Headache?"

"No. More of a preventative measure. I don't want to flake out on you this afternoon."

We ride the rest of the way in relative silence, Cameron absent-mindedly rubbing the back of my hand with his thumb, me thrilling at the flutter of emotions that course through me with every caress. I'm not used to feeling this way about someone. I don't know if that's why I pushed the other boys away, or if it really was because I was worried about them finding out about me, but for the first time I'm wishing I can tell someone about the flickering.

Careful not to turn my head, I glance at Cameron out of the corner of my eye. His left hand rests loosely on the steering wheel, his gaze trained on the road. He's the only boy I trust—and that came long before I had any feelings for him. Maybe I can trust him with this, too.

I clear my throat. "Cam?"

"Yeah?" He slides his hand up my arm and turns to look at me.

It's too soon. What the hell am I thinking?

"Biz?"

"I want to tell you—"

His phone rings. His hand moves to his pocket but he doesn't answer. He's waiting for me to finish.

Not gonna happen.

It rings again.

"Do you need to get that?"

He checks the display and sighs before answering. "Hey, mom." His grip on the steering wheel tightens as he listens. The color fades from his face and the muscle in his jaw trembles.

I touch his arm.

"Did the police call you?"

My head whips up. "What happened?" I whisper.

He shakes his head at me. "We're on our way to the football game." He listens. "I can't. I have to take pictures for a project that's due next week."

It must not be that serious if he doesn't have to go home

right away.

He glances at me, then back at the road. "Maybe we can leave a little early." I nod emphatically and he attempts a smile. His mouth wobbles and his voice cracks. "I love you, too."

I force myself not to pounce the second he hangs up. Three deep breaths later, I speak. "What now?"

He runs his free hand through his hair and a tear slips down his face. "Another girl is missing."

My stomach rolls. "When?"

"This morning."

"Why did the police—" I stop. I already know why the police called his parents.

"It's not about me. They think it's connected to Katie."

I stumble for the right thing to say but come up empty-handed. "We can go back. Turner will give you an extension."

"And tell him I'm crying over some kid I don't even know?" His voice breaks again and the car veers onto the shoulder. He presses harder on the gas. Gravel kicks up on the side of the road.

A flutter of panic makes me sit upright. "Do you want me to drive?"

He swerves into the opposite lane.

"Cam!"

The car straightens and we slow to a normal speed. "Sorry."

"You're freaking me out." I have a weird sense of reverse déjà vu. How many times have we had this same conversation, except I'm the one scaring him? "Are you sure you're okay to drive?"

"Biz, I'd never let anything happen to you." The color is starting to come back to his face but his eyes are a little too wide, making him look a little deranged.

"I know you wouldn't on purpose, but it was like I lost you there for a second." Again, same words, different person saying them.

"I'm okay." He rolls his shoulders and tilts his head from side to side the way a boxer does before entering the ring. Thanks, Dad, for shoving that bit of knowledge into my brain. "But would you mind if we leave at halftime?"

"Of course." I'm a little disappointed that we won't have as much time together, but it's not like I won't see him again. "Do you still want me to come over tomorrow?"

A frustrated sigh fills the air between us. "I don't know. Can I tell you in the morning? I have a feeling tonight's gonna be bad."

Okay, now I'm officially upset and we aren't even at the game yet.

"Hey," he grabs my hand. "I want to see you. You're practically all I think about. I just don't know with my parents."

"It's not fair for them to basically ground you because of all this."

He raises an eyebrow and I cringe.

I despise whiney girls and here I am acting like a two-year old. "You know what I mean. What do you do with them anyway? Do you sit around and talk about her?"

He pulls his hand away. "I just try to be there for them. You know, help out more around the house. It's sad for me, but for them it's like reliving her disappearance all over again."

"It's not like that for you?" I try to eat the words but they're already out. Am I dense? "I'm sorry I'm being an ass. This isn't coming out right." I take off my sunglasses, flickering be damned. "I'm genuinely wondering what you do at home with them, I'm not—"

He stares straight ahead.

Shit.

When we get to the school I consider staying in the car. Cameron didn't speak for the last five minutes and I'm terrified to open my mouth in case more nonsense spews from me.

He climbs out.

I don't move.

He sticks his head through the open door. "You coming?"

"Are you sure you want me to? I seem to have misplaced the filter between my brain and my mouth."

That earns a grin.

"I'm sorry for earlier. I just—"

"Don't worry about it. It's not you I'm mad at; it's this fucking guy..."

I really am a girl. He's thinking about the kidnapper and the horrible things he's doing to these girls and probably did to his sister, and I'm stressing about whether or not he's mad at me. I get out of the car. Cameron grabs our camera bags and we walk hand in hand to the stadium.

Once inside, we stare up at the looming bleachers. They're double the size of the ones at our school and every square inch is filled with purple and gold.

Cameron snorts. "What was that you said about school spirit?"

"There's no lack of spirit here, that's for sure."

"Do you wanna stake out a spot or just wander around?"

My legs are stiff from the ride and although it's bright out, the sun feels good on my face. "Let's walk around. Maybe we can get what we need in the first period and be done with it."

"Quarter."

"Huh?"

"Football has quarters."

I roll my eyes. This is not information I need to know. I lead him along the path in front of the bleachers and scan the crowd for any of our friends. A few familiar faces pop out at me but most of our friends don't go to home games—there's no way they'd trek to an away game. Two girls from our photo class wave from the third row, and Turner himself is sitting a couple rows back. "Turner's here."

Cameron looks up. "Checking up on us?"

"That doesn't seem like his style, but you never know." My conversation with Turner about getting photos published comes to mind. Maybe he's here to make extra money.

We stop at the end of the bleachers and turn to face the field. Guys my age should not wear spandex. Ever. Yet there they are, bent at the waist, their junk on display for everyone in the stands. "Ugh."

"I can't tell you how happy it makes me to hear you say that."

"Can't they wear sweats or something?"

"It's got something to do with aerodynamics. At least that's what I tell myself. You'll never catch me in pants like that." Cameron unzips his bag and pulls out his camera.

I do the same just as a whistle blows.

Woo-hoo. Let the fun begin.

Chapter 18

Football is a lot noisier than soccer. The whistle blows ten times as often, the players insist on slamming their helmets together every chance they get, and every person in the stadium screams any time the ball moves. I follow the same routine as before and take two dozen pictures before the end of the first quarter. I guess it doesn't matter much what I'm shooting once I get into it.

Cameron clicks away beside me, his steady breathing the only calming thing around me.

"You getting anything good?"

He presses a button and shows me his display.

My mouth drops open. "Cam, those are great."

He zoomed so close on the players that you can see the sweat through bars in their facemasks. In another series, he captured their backs when they were all lined up and crouched at the line.

I punch him lightly when I see the next one. It's me, focused on the field.

"I couldn't help myself. We've spent all this time taking pictures for class and I don't have any recent ones of you."

"Well then let me return the favor." I shift to face his and his lips fill the frame. Okay, maybe I better zoom out. His face fills the display and I press the button. I widen the shot further, focusing on the crowd behind him so his face goes blurry. Click-click-click. Something at the edge of the frame catches my eye. I point slightly over Cameron's shoulder and zoom in on the crowd. "It's him."

"Him who?"

"That man."

Cameron twists around and places a hand on my camera. "Show me."

I switch to display mode and the man stares back at us.

Cameron stands up and pulls me to my feet. "We need to tell someone."

"Cam, wait. He's probably someone's dad. It's not like I've

seen him anyplace other than games."

"How many kids does this guy have that he's been at three different sports? We don't have that many big families in our school."

He's convincing, but I feel weird telling on someone who hasn't actually done anything. Wait, Turner's here. "We could talk to Turner. He'd know if that man's a parent."

Cameron's already walking towards the stands.

"Hey, kids." Turner rises when he sees us. The people next to him slide down and we squeeze onto the bench. "Having fun?"

I nod, surprised. I am having fun. Not because of what's going on out on the field, but time seems to slip away when I'm taking pictures. "Yeah, Cam's got some really good shots."

Turner takes Cameron's proffered camera and flips through the images. "Cameron, these are really impressive. I don't know if Biz told you that I've been encouraging her to try to get her photographs published in the local paper, but apparently I need to have that same conversation with you."

Cameron lowers his head so his hair falls in his face, his reaction when anyone says something nice to him. "Yeah, maybe." He clears his throat. "But that's not why we came over here." He nods at me and I shake my head.

Turner looks back and forth between us, waiting. It's like he's got my dad's manual.

I exhale dramatically. "It's probably nothing, but Cam thinks we should tell someone." I pause. Tattling is such a childish reaction. It's not like the guy did anything. Why are we even—

"Well I'm here. Tell me." Turner looks me in the eye, oblivious to the shouts and screams that surround us.

I look over his shoulder, but there's nothing out of the ordinary. Now I'm just stalling.

"Biz, just tell him."

I take another deep breath and spit it out. "There's this man who I keep seeing at the games. Nothing happened but he kinda freaks me out the way I keep catching him watching me. And he's always alone. He's gotta be someone's dad, because why else would he be there, right?" Saying the words out loud makes this whole thing sound even more ridiculous.

Turner leans his elbows on his knees. "When you say he freaks you out, how do you mean? Has he said something or looked at you strangely?"

I think back to the past couple games. "He definitely hasn't talked to me, but it was creepy how I'd see him through my viewfinder and he'd be looking at me. But I'm sure he was just watching me take pictures. I mean, how many high school kids have a camera like mine?"

Cameron scoffs. "That makes no sense and you know it." He touches my back and gently traces his fingers over my shoulder blades. "Stop making excuses. He scared you, that's why I wanted you to tell someone."

"What made you decide to tell me right now?" Turner asks.

"Because I saw him again."

"Here?"

"Yeah, just a few minutes ago. We were taking pictures near the side of the field."

"Right, I saw you there."

"And when I turned to the crowd he was there. I told Cam, but when I looked back to where I'd seen him, he was gone."

"Did he see you?"

The memory of the way the man's dark eyes seemed to disappear inside his skull sends a chill through me. "Yeah. I'm pretty sure."

Turner seems to choose his words carefully. "Is there any

chance you got a picture of him?"

My camera weighs heavily in my lap. "Yeah, at the soccer game on Tuesday. I didn't mean to, but he was in the frame."

His eyes drop to my camera. "Any chance it's still on there?"

I shake my head. "No, I delete them after they download. I can bring in a flash drive on Monday."

"Can you email it to me instead?"

"Uh, sure." The anxious expression on Turner's face makes my head spin. I had myself convinced that I was overreacting and figured Turner would tell us to stop causing trouble. I never expected him to validate our concerns.

Turner pulls a business card out of his wallet and hands it to me. "Could you send it to me tonight?"

Cameron sits up straight. "Are you saying this guy's up to something?"

"I don't know, but given the events over the past week, I think it's smart to look into every possibility." Turner looks at me. "You know my friend at the newspaper?"

I nod.

"Her husband's a cop."

Cameron's mouth drops open. "We're not saying he did

anything. I don't want to accuse him of anything."

Turner's face softens. "Cameron, relax. I'm going to pass the photo along and they can choose to do with it as they wish. I'd be remiss to ignore the intuition of two of my favorite students."

A sudden rush of heat stalls my words in my throat. Favorite students?

Cameron recovers more smoothly. "Will you let us know what they say?"

"I'm sure it will be nothing, but I'll pass along anything worth repeating."

That doesn't sound like a yes to me. Before I can protest a whistle blows and people rise all around us. Including Turner.

"Do either of you need anything from the concession stand? I'm heading that way."

Cameron stands as well. "No, thanks. We're gonna cut out a little early. My parents want me home because of the other kidnapping."

Turner falters, a movement so subtle I almost miss it. But his rapidly paling face is more noticeable. "There... there's been another one?" The shift in his mood is startling, as if

Cameron's words unplugged whatever normally keeps Turner in go-go-go mode and left a shell of our teacher standing in front of us.

Cameron glances at me and I shrug my shoulders. I have no idea why Turner's reacting like this. Cameron touches his arm. "Maybe you should sit down."

I jump to my feet, my home-made emergency training kicking in. "Or do you want us to get you a drink? Maybe some candy?" Turner sinks onto the bench and I touch his forehead, then quickly pull my hand back. He's my teacher. I don't think we're allowed to touch.

"No, you kids go on. I'll be fine."

"No offense," Cameron says, "but you don't look fine." We exchange puzzled looks over Turner's head, and for the second time in fifteen minutes I find myself wondering if we should tell an adult what's going on.

Turner presses his hand to his chest and studies us with watery eyes. "You just caught me off guard." He looks off toward the field, then at Cameron. "It gets easier, but you'll never forget."

Cameron's lips tighten into a firm line. They seem to have

an understanding, but I have no clue what it's about.

I bite my tongue when we say goodbye to Turner and keep my mouth shut during the walk through the parking lot, but now that we're in the car and driving home, I can't stop myself. "What the hell happened back there?"

"You don't remember?"

"Clearly I don't." Cameron winces, and I'm left feeling like I should know about this secret bond the two of them apparently have. I tone down the attitude. "Can you please tell me what's going on? The only adult I know who goes all wobbly like that is my dad, and I know Turner doesn't have epilepsy."

Cameron snorts, which sends my blood pressure soaring. "No, nothing like that." He takes a quick breath. "When Katie had been gone for a couple months, someone from the police department recommended this support group for families of people who'd gone missing."

"Like AA?"

"Yeah, sort of. Anyway, my mom didn't want to go. She kept insisting that Katie would come home and it would be a waste of time to learn how to get along without her."

I vaguely remember Cameron telling me about this when

it happened. "You and your dad went, right?"

"Only once. It was too depressing sitting in a room with all these people who were missing someone." He switches hands on the steering wheel and rests a hand on mine. "I didn't make the connection until just now, but Turner was at that meeting."

My head whips towards him. "As part of the support group?"

"Yeah."

I wait for him to continue, but he's staring at the road, lost in his memories. I hate to interrupt, but... "Do you know who disappeared?"

He remains silent for so long I start to wonder if I spoke out loud, but he turns his head slightly to look at me, fresh tears in his eyes. "I think it was his daughter."

His words slam me back against my seat. "Holy shit. I had no idea."

"I'd completely forgotten he was there. It's not like I knew him back then, and I've sort of blocked out a lot of what happened after Katie disappeared."

Helplessness makes my chest feel heavy, solid. Each time I think I understand how deeply Cameron was affected by Katie's disappearance, he shows me a little bit more. I don't know if I'd have the strength to get on with my life the way he has. I stare at my hand beneath his. "I don't know how you do it."

His thumb twitches over my fingers. "Some days I don't either."

I curl my fingers through his, hoping the small gesture in some way shows that I care. "You know words aren't my thing—I'd much rather take a picture to show how I'm feeling—but I want you to know that I'm here for you. If there's anything at all I can do..."

He lifts my hand to his mouth and grazes my fingers with his lips. "I know, Biz. That's why I'm here."

◆ ◆ ◆

Headlights from an oncoming car fill Old Berta's interior as we turn into my neighborhood, but the sense of dread that follows me at dusk lifts. I allow myself to relax. I won't be flickering today.

Cameron touches the side of my face and I turn to look at him. "I wish I could hang out, but I need to get home."

"Will you let me know what your parents say about tomorrow?"

He parks at the end of my driveway and kills the engine. "I'll text you tonight. Now come here." His seatbelt clicks and he leans across the space between us, enveloping me in his arms.

I breathe in the musky scent that seems to seep from his pores, a mixture of vanilla soap and outdoors, and tuck my forehead against his warm neck. We stay that way for a few minutes, our heartbeats synchronized. Too soon I feel him stir against me and I pull back.

His eyes are bloodshot and his mouth is set in a hard line. Apparently he wasn't thinking the same lovey-dovey things I was.

I lean against my seat and he rests an arm on the steering wheel. "Do you want to talk about it?"

"No. I should go." He sighs. "Besides, there isn't anything to talk about."

I lean towards him once again and rest my hand on the side of his face. His jaw clenches beneath my touch. I pull him closer and press a light kiss on his lips. "Good night." I'm hoping he'll pull me back and tell me to stay a little longer, but his hand doesn't leave the dashboard.

"Good night."

I climb out of the car and grab my bag from the backseat

before running to the house. The dread lifts even further when I realize all the downstairs lights are on. My parents are home. No one went to the ER. I turn to wave at Cameron, then open the front door as he drives down the street.

"Hello?" I drop my bag at the foot of the stairs.

My parents are in the living room watching television. Mom mutes the sound when I come in. "How was the game?"

"Fine." I look between her and Dad, then back to the television. She muted Jeopardy. This must be important. "What's up?"

Their concern is palpable. Mom won't stop pulling on the hem of her sleeve and Dad's crossed and uncrossed his legs three times since I walked into the room. And the television is still silent. I run through the list of reasons why they could be upset with me, but nothing major stands out. Curiosity urges me to press them, but I wait. I'm learning.

After what feels like an hour, Dad sits forward. "Another girl disappeared."

"Oh, that." I sigh audibly and they both raise an eyebrow.

"Oh that?" Mom echoes.

I sit on the edge of the couch. "Cam's mom called to

tell him right after we left school. I thought this was about something else."

"Like what?"

"Nothing, I just—were you just going to tell me about her, or is there something else?"

Dad looks at Mom and she clears her throat. "We're worried about the hours you keep. Especially the early drives. We know you like to take photos then—" that's what I have them thinking "—but we're afraid something could happen to you."

My mind scrambles to come up with a good excuse. I can't blow them off about something this serious, but how do I convince them that I'm not in danger? "It's only been little kids who've been taken, and it's when they're running around outside, right?" They both scowl. Okay, maybe that wasn't the best approach. "I'm just saying, I'm in my car and driving. How would someone talk to me, let alone try to kidnap me?"

Mom sighs, a long, drawn out exhalation of breath that seems to wrap around the room. Maybe I've convinced them. "Biz, we know you're almost an adult and can take care of yourself, but you are still our baby. We can't help but worry."

"I always have my phone. If someone ever tries to stop me

I promise to call you right away."

This time Dad sighs, and I know I've won. That seemed a little too easy, but I'll take it.

But I don't want to rub their faces in it. "Are we okay? I don't want to make you guys worry, but I really don't think I'm in any danger." I get up and give Mom a quick hug, then linger a bit with Dad. "I swear I'll be safe."

With that over, I head upstairs and grab my camera from my bag. Turner's business card flutters to the floor. I finger the edge, Cameron's words flooding back to me. I can't believe that something so awful happened to Turner and I never knew. With Cameron, it's like his sister's disappearance is a badge he wears, not necessarily out of obligation, but as a way to never forget her, and it surprises me that there's this side to Turner I'd never imagined.

I set his card next to my computer and scroll through my images from the past week. Trace fills my screen, followed by a distant shot of his teammates gathered around their coach, and then my breath catches. The man is staring at me. This isn't the first time I've seen this photo since uploading them, but the intensity in his gaze freaks me out. I lean closer, studying the lines around his deep-set eyes and the way his light hair brushes the top of his ears.

How is it that he was looking right at me when I took the picture? The thought of him watching us when we weren't paying attention to him makes my skin crawl. A shimmer of concern pricks the back of my neck. Maybe my parents are right to be worried.

I open my email and type in Turner's address, attach the photo, and click send.

I'm halfway through the photos from the football game when Cameron texts.

"They said no."

Ugh. "Why?"

Silence.

"Hello?"

"They don't want company right now."

"Since when am I company?"

I've been hanging out at his house since we were in elementary school. I'd shed the company label around the same time I ditched my pigtails and rainbow sneakers. Or so I thought.

More silence.

Guilt burns my chest. Cameron's dealing with a lot of shit and I'm stressing over a stupid label. "Are you okay?"

Still nothing.

Well, crap.

Chapter 19

My alarm goes off long before the sun rises—I set it on vibrate so I won't wake my parents—and I'm pretty sure I'm the only person in my high school anxious to roll out of bed right now. I slip into yesterday's jeans and tug on a sweatshirt before tip-toeing down the hall.

Dad's snoring drifts through their closed door, but that's it. No tell-tale light that they're awake.

Downstairs I grab an apple from the bottom drawer of the fridge then sneak out the door.

Streaks of red and orange light the sky as I head towards the Strand. I take a few bites of the apple, then toss it on the floor of the passenger seat. I'm not hungry, and while I can't say I've ever noticed if they affect my migraines, I figure it can't hurt.

I round a bend and the Strand looms up ahead, but the sun isn't high enough yet.

This happens sometimes. Because the time of the sunrise changes, I don't always get here at the right moment. Once last winter I was so early I killed time drinking coffee at a diner. But I think a quick loop to the next main road and back should give the sun a chance to do its thing.

I drive slowly to the next bend in the road. For a second I consider stopping on the shoulder, but my promise to my parents urges me to keep moving. Barely ten hours have passed since they asked me to be careful, and here I am contemplating doing exactly what worries them.

No matter. A burst of light breaks the tree line. It's time.

I check the rearview mirror to make sure no one's behind me, then press the accelerator. It doesn't matter if anyone's here, but I don't really know what happens to my car when I flicker. I assume it's like a big rewind button freezes everything, then whips everything back to yesterday, but images of my car careening into a ditch or skidding into oncoming traffic make me avoid other cars if I can.

Slivers of light shine though the trees. I roll down the window. The cool air lifts my hair and sharpens my senses.

I flex my fingers, allowing the tingling to sweep through my arms and out my toes. I take a deep breath. The heaviness pushes me back and I struggle to control the car. Lower, lower, I sink into the seat, my gaze barely clearing the dashboard, my fingers slipping from the steering wheel… and the weight vanishes and I'm sitting upright, my feet drifting from the pedals. I turn my head to glance at the trees and—

I'm walking down the hall with Amelia, heading to lunch.

Bishop's class isn't as bad this time around since I already know about the ridiculous score on my test, but I'd love to skip his pep talk. I'm a little calmer when Cameron and I leave for the football game, but knowing what happens doesn't calm the butterflies. Repeating things doesn't seem to have an effect on them.

When Cameron's mom calls I turn away so my expression doesn't reveal anything, when a feeling of horror more intense than anything I've ever felt slams into me. The girl just got kidnapped.

And I knew about it.

I try to act surprised when Cameron tells me the news, but

I can't get past the turmoil that's shredding my insides. Why why why didn't I do anything? I could have called one of those anonymous tip lines or… I don't know, gone to her house or something. Anything. Now she's gone.

Fortunately Cameron's so distracted he hasn't noticed that I've yet to say anything. We ride in silence until we arrive at the stadium.

Cameron turns off the car and reaches over to touch the back of my neck. "You've been quiet. Is your headache back?"

I touch my temple. "Yeah, a little." I worry that lying to him will somehow jinx me, then remember it will: I've already flickered so I've got about twelve hours until it descends.

I follow Cameron through the parking lot and let him pick the far corner to get settled. My energy rebounds a little when I start taking pictures, and I almost forget about the creepy man. I turn towards the stands. It'd probably be better to email Turner a more recent picture of this guy.

He's sitting right where I saw him, but for once he isn't watching me. I follow his gaze to the field. Maybe he is someone's dad and it's just a coincidence that I keep catching him staring.

Cameron's shutter clicks next to me and I quickly take a dozen shots of the man. As if he senses me, his head slowly turns my way until his eyes are holding mine. A shiver runs down my spine and I lean closer to Cameron.

He slides his free arm around me. "What's wrong?"

"That man is here again." I point him out and I'm halfway to my feet when Cameron stands.

"We need to tell someone."

"He's probably someone's dad. It's not like I've seen him anyplace other than games." My heart isn't in it this time. I know we need to talk to Turner, but I don't like changing things more than I need to. In this case I feel like I need to let Cameron convince me. Give him something to think about other than kidnappings.

"How many kids does this guy have that he's been at three different sports? We don't have that many big families in our school."

I pause long enough to make him believe I'm considering his argument. "We could talk to Turner. He'd know if this man is someone's parent."

Cameron's already walking towards the stands.

The conversation with Turner goes much the same way, except this time I have pictures to show him.

"I've never seen him before. I don't attend every game, but I'm fairly certain I'd recognize a parent. Biz, do you mind emailing these to me tonight when you get home?"

I nod and accept his card.

The drive home is quiet and I wait for Cameron's promise to text me later before climbing out of the car. If he senses my distance he doesn't call me out on it, but he's had years of practice.

I take a deep breath, steeling myself for the talk with my parents. I fling open the door. "I'm home."

They're in the living room, looking nervous. I let them start.

Dad sits forward. "Another girl disappeared."

"I heard. Cameron's mom called while we at the game."

Dad looks at Mom and she clears her throat. "We're worried about the hours you keep. Especially the early drives. We know you like to take photos then but we're afraid something could happen to you."

"But if I'm driving, how could someone do anything? I swear I'm careful." I'm feeling especially guilty since the reason I'm repeating this conversation is because of my early morning drive yesterday. Tomorrow. I shake my head. It's sometimes hard to keep track of the days.

Mom sighs.

Repeating lectures is the worst part of flickering. No, repeating classes is the worst part, but this is a close second. Why couldn't Cameron have kissed me before he dropped me off? That I'd like to do over. And over.

"Biz, we know you're almost an adult and can take care of yourself, but you are still our baby. We can't help but worry about you."

"I always have my phone. If someone ever tries to stop me I promise to call you right away."

Dad sighs.

I give them another minute. "Are we okay? I don't want to make you guys worry, but I really don't think it's a big deal." I get up and give Mom a quick hug, then linger a bit with Dad. "I swear I'll be safe."

I run upstairs to email Turner and wait for Cameron's text. If only there was a way to change his parents' decision.

◆ ◆ ◆

I toss my phone across the room.

You'd think it'd hurt less to hear I can't go to Cameron's tomorrow since I already knew that's what would happen, but it doesn't. An unfamiliar longing sweeps through me, crushing me, curling me into a ball on my bed. Then it pisses me off.

I sit up. He's a guy. A guy. Why am I letting myself get so worked up over him? I'd never admit it, but I pride myself on not getting hung up on boys.

But Cameron's different, a little voice insists, and I curl back up.

I allow myself to wallow for a few minutes, then the voice shifts. I need to know about the little girl. I pull my laptop off my desk and rest it on my pillow. A couple of keystrokes later she's staring back at me. Brown hair, brown eyes, missing front tooth.

My stomach turns and I close my eyes. I'm so fucking stupid. Why didn't I think of her sooner when I could have actually done something to help? I scroll down, my finger slowly moving over the touchpad until her freckles are gone. The words swim by; bits of information that could have been useful if I'd bothered to look it up last night. My finger stops. The police say there's definitely a connection with Katie. They're reopening her case.

I don't know if that's a good thing or not. I mean it's good if they can find out what happened to her, but I don't know if Cameron and his parents have the strength to go through all that again. Sometimes it seems like they're barely getting by now.

My gaze drifts to my phone. This explains why they don't want me over there. I roll over and grab my camera from the floor. I refuse to mope any longer. I need to go through my photos and I've only got—I check the clock—less than eight hours before the migraine hits.

An energy zips through me as I start downloading my pictures. I love how immediate photography is. Turner keeps threatening to make us mess around with actual film so we have a 'proper understanding of photography's beginnings blah blah', but it's the immediacy that draws me to it. Mom says I'm always rushing and can't sit still long enough to appreciate anything, but that's not true. I can sit for hours trying to perfectly capture a moment, which is tricky considering the moment is always changing, but once I've got the shot, I want to see it now.

I pause on a shot of several players hunched on the bench. Their slumped shoulders speak more about their displeasure for being stuck there than the scowls on their faces, but I've managed to capture both. Regardless, there's still something missing. It seems flat.

I skip to the next couple shots and my breath catches. That's it. I'd shifted my position so the overhead lights cast a stronger shadow on their faces, masking their unhappiness in darkness while at the same time revealing it to me. I try to recall if I'd made the adjustment intentionally. Yes, yes, of course you did, my ego insists, but I can't take credit for a fluke. I mean, I will take credit for it, obviously, but I know this effect wasn't on purpose.

I hide the photo application and double-click a text file saved to my desktop. I scroll to the bottom of the list and type 'include shadows'. Several items near the top of the list have a line through them—those reminders are already second nature—but I'm still working on the others. I reread the list, starting at the bottom.

Tighter composition.

Drastic angles.

Stop making people smile.

Faster setting for action.

My last thoughts before falling asleep are a mix of irony and relief. Irony that I don't care enough about most of my other classes to try this hard, and relief that I care about something enough to try.

Chapter 20

The ice picks wake me up again. My eyes scrunch tighter. The pillow already cocoons my head, but I pull it closer, trying to block out the inevitable.

The smell of bacon drifts upstairs and my stomach heaves. Acid churns in my stomach and the juices in my mouth start flowing. I yank the pillow off my head and fall out of bed. I haven't thrown up in awhile, but it looks like today is my lucky day.

Fortunately the bathroom's close.

I flush, then tiptoe back to bed. Mom knows better than to expect me for breakfast on the weekend, but I'd rather she not know about this headache. She's got enough to worry about with Dad.

I cower deeper under the covers as the room grows brighter and brighter.

"Biz, honey? You getting up?" Mom's voice drifts through the layers of cotton and feathers.

"Ughhhhh."

My door clicks open and glass clinks on wood. "I brought you some apple juice and toast. There's a pill next to the glass."

I raise a corner of the blanket and peek at Mom. "How did you know?"

She sits on the edge of the bed and slides a cool hand beneath the blankets, searching for my tender neck. Her fingers dig into the knots at the base of my skull. "I'm your mother. You think I don't know when you're sick?"

My eyes close as she kneads the tendon beneath my ear. I'd purr if I didn't think it'd make my head fall off.

She continues until my breathing slows, then presses a kiss to my temple.

"Thanks, Mom."

The pill touches my lips. "Drink up." A straw juts from the glass.

I catch it with my lips, swallow.

The pill does its thing and knocks me out for a couple more

hours, until my phone dings. My hand shoots out from the covers to put it on silent.

Don't check it. Keep sleeping.

But what if it's him?

I peek at the display. It's Cameron, apologizing again.

I call him instead of texting back. That way I can keep my eyes closed. "It's okay. I read about Katie's case being opened back up."

He's quiet for a minute. A clock ticks in the background. He must be in the kitchen. "Yeah." He says something else, but my mind wanders, the hazy loops of the medication clouding my thoughts and making me completely space out.

"What?"

He sighs, an angry sound that I don't expect. "Why did you call if you don't wanna talk?"

My eyes snap open. My stomach plummets. "I feel like ass and didn't want to have to look at my phone."

"Well I've got a lot on my mind right now."

"What? Cam—"

"Forget it."

I think he's hung up but I can still hear the clock ticking. "Cam?"

One more sigh and the line goes silent. He's hung up.

Everything goes liquid inside and I run to the bathroom.

◆ ◆ ◆

Shadows creep across the wall. When dusk erases the last bits of color from the room, I roll out of bed. I do still have homework.

My computer whirs to life. I slide my finger over the trackpad and freeze. The picture of the man at the soccer game stares back at me. I quickly flip backwards until I find a shot I like, then save it in a folder for my project. If I use two photos from each game, plus the feature section on Trace, I won't need to write much. Turner can't actually expect us to have full articles.

I save a couple more, the layout for the page arranging itself in my head, but my finger pauses over the folder for the football game. Cameron hasn't called or texted. I double-click the folder and sigh in relief. It's just the game. I couldn't remember if I'd taken a couple of him—crap, there's one of him focusing on the players on the bench. It's probably the same shot I was admiring earlier, but better. The ache in my stomach gets worse. "Not now." I press a hand against my belly and try to focus on the pictures. Maybe I should just delete the ones of him so I won't have to keep looking at his face.

A flutter in my throat surprises me. Not really a flutter, but a knot that makes it hard to swallow. What the hell? My eyes start to burn. "Are you kidding me?" I don't cry over boys. Not even if they are as wonderful and beautiful and hilarious as Cameron. I clear my throat and quickly click through the rest of the pictures, saving two without really paying attention to which ones I've chosen.

I take more care with the layout of the page. Even with my head staging a mutiny and my emotions urging me back into bed, I want to do well on this project. Besides, I've never let a migraine stop me before.

The design comes together easily—I group the photos from each game, overlapping a tighter action shot over one that covers more of the field, and add a colored section for Trace's interview—but the story itself won't budge. I know what happened, I was there, but sentences refuse to form.

My gaze shifts to the closed door. Maybe Dad can help.

I creep down the stairs as fast as I can without causing my brain to leak out of my ear. The scent of roasted chicken and mashed potatoes wafts from the kitchen. My comfort food.

Mom and Dad look up from the television when I enter the room. Mom smiles. "We weren't sure if we'd see you today. Are you feeling any better?"

I shrug, and hope they don't push it. I hate dwelling on my limitations. I face Dad. "I need help with my photo project."

He sighs, a weary sound that seems to deflate him. I notice for the first time how withered he looks.

"Are you okay?" I look between him and Mom.

He ignores my question. "You need my help with a photo project? You know far more than me."

"It's not the photos, it's the writing." I explain the project and give him my best puppy dog eyes. Which given how crappy I feel, isn't difficult.

"Can you bring your computer down here?"

Mom trails her fingers over his shoulder, trying to be casual, but I see her check his pulse.

"What's going on?"

"I'm just more tired than normal. Nothing to worry about." I've heard that line before. "Go get your computer and we'll work on this while Mom finishes up dinner."

"Are you sure?"

He squeezes my knee. "Stop babying me."

I hurry upstairs, wincing on each step, then return with my computer and a notepad, which I hand to Dad. He hates computers. I point at the screen. "I have the pictures figured out, but I'm supposed to write a story to go along with it."

He considers the images, the pencil lodged firmly between his teeth. He traces the edge of a shadow with his finger and sets the pencil on the couch next to him. "I really like the way you've worked the shadows into each shot."

I resist the urge to slap his hand off the monitor and wait for him to finish his thought.

"But that's probably not a good angle, huh?" He chuckles at his pun and I roll my eyes. "You could tell a story from the perspective of a non-sports fan." He pokes my side. "A stretch, I know. Explain that even though you don't understand the rules, you can still appreciate the determination and hard work." He pauses. "Do you appreciate that?"

I look down. How did he manage to work a lecture into this? "I'm trying Dad."

He touches my cheek. "I don't want you to miss opportunities. You never know when things could change. I know it

seems like you've got your whole life in front of you, but…"
He shakes his head.

"Is that what happened with you?"

He waves his hands at his body, his lip curled with displeasure.
"I wasn't always like this. I went out with friends, went to work, helped around the house." He sighs. "I worry that I'm setting a bad example for you because you never knew the person I was."

"So you didn't always have seizures?" Over the years I'd picked up that they started after he and Mom got married, but I'd never asked for details. Now I'm realizing maybe I should have.

His eyes close and he leans back. "No, I didn't." He turns his head to look at me. "They started the night you were born."

My mouth drops. "What do you mean?" I knew he hadn't always had them, but I had no idea they were that closely tied to me.

"Just what I said. I never had a seizure before you were born." His lips press tightly together, like he wants to say more.

I wait.

His eyes never leave mine, but he doesn't continue.

"Did I somehow…" I can't finish. I don't think I want to know if I somehow caused him to be sick. It makes absolutely no sense.

"No!" He grabs my hand. "Biz, no. It isn't your fault." He lets go and his head droops. "It's mine." The last words come out so softly I wonder if he actually said them.

"Your fault?"

Tears glisten in his eyes. "I didn't know that would happen."

"You've lost me."

"I know. I'm sorry." He closes his eyes for a moment and rubs the back of his neck. "How frequently do you get headaches?"

The sudden change in topic catches me off-guard. "I don't know." Just when I flicker. "Why?"

He stares past me, unfocused. "I got headaches when I was your age, too."

My heart stutters.

"I remember how awful they were, and I hate to think that you're suffering that way. I know you don't tell us every time you have one, and I wish there was a way I could make it... less excruciating."

That's a good word.

"If it's ever more than you can handle, will you tell me?"

No. "Of course."

"I'm serious, Biz."

"I know." I lean forward to accept his embrace. "Thanks, Dad."

His grip tightens. "I know you don't like to hear it, but I worry about you. More than you know."

I pull away. I love my dad and it means a lot to me that he cares so much—most of my friends don't have that kind of relationship with their parents—but tonight he's hit a little too close to the truth.

"Thanks, Dad." I gather my stuff and leave him on the couch. Upstairs, I shut my door and flop onto the bed.

I still have no idea what to write for my project.

Chapter 21

As a rule, Mondays suck. But this Monday sucks more than usual because it's the first time I'm nervous about turning in a photo project. Plus I still have lingering effects from my headache. And Cameron's not in school.

The day passes in a blur. My friends know enough about my headaches to give me space when I feel like crap, but I make an effort not to dump my shitty mood all over them. Everyone's too distracted by the second kidnapping to pay much attention to me anyways.

One small blessing: I get to skip Trig today. The bad news: it's for another assembly. The police are back to talk to us about safety and juniors get to miss fifth period. I sit next to Amelia and we pass the time coming up with reasons why Cameron isn't here today.

"I get that his parents are upset, but why would he stay home?" Amelia wonders. "I mean, do they sit in a circle being all sad, or what?"

"I asked him that." Or did I? I think I managed to keep that comment to myself the second time around.

Her mouth drops. "You did not. What did he say?"

"He didn't react very well."

"I bet."

"I wonder what will happen now that the police have said there's a connection between these kids and Katie."

"I didn't hear that."

I nod at the stage. "Maybe we should actually pay attention." Since Cameron isn't talking to me this might give me a little more understanding about what Cameron's going through.

Amelia shrugs, and a shudder passed through me. Is anyone else is aware of Cameron's absence? A surge of protectiveness sharpens my focus; I want to shield him from the police, from the rumors, from ever suffering like that again.

Stride Right comes back on stage. "I know you think this has nothing to do with you, but we're all a part of this community, and what happens to one or two or three families affects us all." Several people snicker and Stride Right scowls. His 'community' talk gets a little old. "This is important. Someone is taking our children and it makes me sick to think that tomorrow it might be one of you."

That shuts everyone up.

We file out quietly. My thoughts are on Katie and the chaos those first days after she disappeared. Are these other families going through the same thing? From the dejected expressions on my classmates' faces, I imagine they're thinking the same thing.

The rest of the day passes quickly. We turn in our assignments in photo class, but Turner doesn't have us present them. Instead he introduces the next project.

"Photojournalism, at its core, is about telling stories through photos. The sports page was an introduction to that concept, albeit a limited one. For your next project I'd like you to find something that qualifies as real news. Something you'd see on the front page of the newspaper, as a lead story online, or even on the evening news. I'm not saying you need to become ambulance chasers, and I realize that you're in school most of the day, but you might be surprised at how changing the filter through which you observe the world will open your eyes to things you've previously overlooked."

My mind whirs to life, headache funk be damned. No more sitting on the sidelines at staged events. We're being told to go out and explore. I never would have put it in those words, but based on the physical reaction I'm having, this is exactly what I've been waiting for.

It's like my eyes have been opened. A fog I never realized surrounded me lifts as I'm driving home and I'm seeing things I've never noticed before. An almost accident at the intersection in front of school. An excess of For Sale signs in front of houses. A dead cat on the side of the road. Everything has become a possible story.

I'm eyeing a front door that's been left ajar when my fingers start to tingle.

No!

But it's too late. The flicker comes fast. In the time it takes me to roll down the street, my hands and feet go numb, I'm crushed into the seat, then I'm floating out of my body. My subconscious registers a rubber ball bouncing in front of my car and—

Dad's hugging me on the couch.

Fuck. The hazy dizziness that lingers a day or two after a headache is still there, and now I've gone back again. This is gonna suck. Maybe I can leave school early tomorrow and be home before it hits.

I promise Dad I'll let him know if the headaches get worse, hoping he doesn't notice that I can't look him in the eye and make a mental note to avoid him tomorrow afternoon.

Chapter 22

I convince the school nurse to let me skip my last class and am home in bed, a pill in my gut, when the railroad spike drives through my brain.

Mom knocks on my door a few hours later. "Biz, are you coming down for dinner?"

This is where my acting skills come in. I don't want them to know I have another headache, so I need to act normal. Or close to normal. "I'll be down in a minute." I slowly peel the covers off my head and do a quick mental inventory. Ice pick in skull: check. Dizziness: check. Nausea: not so much.

Maybe I can make it through dinner.

Or not.

Midway through my mashed potatoes my stomach heaves. I sprint up the stairs and make it to the bathroom in time.

Mom's right behind me. "You still have a headache?"

Sure, that works. I nod, my head still draped over the toilet.

"Maybe you should stay home tomorrow."

"Okay."

I crawl back in bed and don't get up again until Amelia calls after school. She knows I won't answer texts when I feel like this.

"So what's up? Are you and Cam playing hooky together?"

A fresh wave of nausea sweeps over me. I still haven't heard from him.

"Biz?"

"He wasn't at school?"

"You haven't talked to him?"

"No."

"Is everything okay with you guys?"

I debate how much to tell her. There isn't much to say. I was a jackass after the football game and now he isn't talking to me. "I'm not sure. I got upset that his parents didn't want me to come over on Saturday and he basically hung up on me."

"And you haven't bothered to call since then?" She knows me better than anyone. "Biz, this is Cam. You can't just blow him off."

"I know."

"I don't think you do. Look," she hesitates. "I'm your friend and I support you when you screw up every relationship you're in, but I love you too much to let you ruin this one."

Ouch.

"You're different with Cam. More yourself than I've ever seen you with a guy, plus you actually seem happy. I don't know what you said to piss him off, but you need to fix it."

My stomach churns, but this time it's not nausea. It's fear. And nerves. And anxiety that Amelia's right and I need to be the one to make things right.

"Hello?"

"You're right. I don't know why I do this, but I don't want to screw this one up." I can hear her smile through the phone. "So, wise one, what do I say to him? This whole begging-for-forgiveness thing is new for me."

"Just tell him you're sorry."

"That's it?" That seems too easy.

"It wouldn't hurt to also tell him how you feel. Not over-the-top mushiness, but guys are just as insecure as we are. They just hide it better. He's probably freaking out about this whole thing."

"When did you learn so much about relationships?"

She giggles. "While you were busy breaking hearts. I've tried to learn from your mistakes."

Double ouch. "Well I'm glad my mistakes are helping one of us."

"Don't be silly. They're helping both of us, it's just taken you a little longer to realize it. Now hang up with me and call Cam."

"Okay, okay. I'll let you know how it goes." I disconnect and call him before I can chicken out, but the phone just rings and rings.

I hang up without leaving a message. That's probably not what Amelia meant.

◆ ◆ ◆

A knock at the door wakes me. The beginnings of a sunrise peek through my curtains. Mom's hand finds my neck beneath the covers, her cool flesh searing my feverish skin.

I roll over and wait for my skull to protest the movement. A vice grips both temples, sending shock waves through my brain and leaving a trail of pinpricks in its wake like my face fell asleep. But the severe stabbing doesn't last.

"Do you think you can make it to school today?"

I push myself onto an elbow. My stomach stays put. I rock my head from side to side, loosening something vital to my equilibrium, but nothing I can't hide from Mom. "I think so. We didn't present our photo projects yet and I'd really like to be there for that." And I don't want to go another day without seeing Cameron.

Mom gives my neck a final squeeze. "I'll have toast waiting for you downstairs."

"Thanks."

I roll out of bed and shove my legs into the closest jeans I see, then pull a sweatshirt from the bottom drawer. I may feel like a railroad spike is stuck in my brain but I refuse to wear a dirty shirt to school. Jeans aren't such a big deal.

The scent of burning toast reaches me in the bathroom. "Thanks, Mom," I mumble. After a quick swipe of goop my hair goes into a ponytail. Done.

My giant sunglasses sit on the counter next to two slices of dry, unburned toast wrapped in a paper towel. Black coffee steams in a travel mug. Guilt edges through my haze. I don't mean to be so ungrateful.

Mom appears in the doorway. "Do you need a ride?"

I slide on my glasses and take a bite of toast, hoping she buys it. "I'll be okay. Thanks for breakfast." I step gingerly through the front door, close the door behind me, then throw up into the bushes.

This is gonna be a long day.

I stumble through school. I haven't seen Cameron but that doesn't mean he's not here. He might just be avoiding me.

"Hey, chica, you look like shit." Amelia sidles up next to me. "I take it you're not eating today?"

My stomach turns just thinking of lunch. "I'll be in the library." Trying to sleep. I could take a nap in the nurse's office, but then she'll want to call my parents and I don't want to get into it with them. The quiet rows between the unused reference books will have to work.

"Okay, I'll see you in Trig." Amelia turns to go, then stops. "Cam's not here?"

My shoulders sag. At least he's not ignoring me. "I haven't seen him."

"What'd he say last night?"

"He didn't answer."

She tilts her head. "And what'd you say in the message you left him, since you surely wouldn't hang up on your boyfriend who you hadn't talked to in two days."

"Uhh…"

"Biz! Please don't screw this up. Call him from the library. No one will be in there anyways."

"Fine."

"You promise?"

She knows I can't break a promise. "Yes."

The table in the far corner of the dusty room calls to me. I settle into a chair so I'm facing the room, then dig my cell phone out of my bag. Cameron still doesn't answer, but this time I wait through the voicemail recording. "Hey, Cam, it's Biz. I just want to make sure you're okay. Text me when you have a minute."

That done, I toss my phone onto the table as my head falls onto my arms.

Chapter 23

"Crap!" I know I set the alarm on my phone, but it never went off. I scramble from the library. The halls are deserted. How many classes did I sleep through?

Looks like I have to go to the nurse's office after all.

I hurry down the hall, crafting an excuse that will cover the fact that I accidentally skipped Trig but keep the nurse from calling Mom.

Becky, the nurse, smiles when she sees me. "Haven't seen you in a couple weeks. How's the noggin?"

"So-so." I hold up my phone. "I took a nap in the library at lunch and my stupid alarm didn't go off."

"What'd you miss?"

"Trig. Bishop."

Becky scribbles on a slip of paper and hands it to me, but doesn't let go when I try to take it. "You know I'm supposed to call your parents."

"I swear I just overslept. I was up late working on homework."

She hesitates. "I don't believe you, but I'll let you go. Do me a favor though?" Her compassionate eyes catch mine. "Please take care of yourself."

"I'm trying."

I head towards Bishop's class, fingering the note. Excused from fifth period. I feel bad for ditching Amelia, but if I'm going to present my project for Turner I need to get my head together. I settle in a stairwell at the end of the hall and mentally run through my project. There isn't much to say. The story part isn't that great, and I'm hoping Turner sticks with what he said and doesn't make that a big percentage of the overall grade. Especially since the pictures turned out really well.

Careful not to fall asleep again, I lean my head against the cool cinderblock wall and let my thoughts wander. They don't go far. Cameron seems to be the first thing I go to the minute

I sit still. I check my phone. Still nothing from him. I start to text, but footsteps sound on the stairs above me and I slip my phone back into my bag.

When the bell rings I throw my bag over my shoulder and make my way to Turner's class. I see Amelia up ahead in the hallway and give her a sheepish look. "Sorry. I fell asleep in the library."

She rolls her eyes. "I need some freakish headache disorder so I can get out of sucky classes too." She hands me a sheet of paper. "Another test tomorrow."

"Great."

She waves goodbye and I let the flow of bodies carry me into Turner's room.

I smile when I see him. He's standing in front of his desk, bouncing on the balls of his feet. A lot of my teachers seem resentful that they have to waste day after day with hundreds of teenagers, but it's like Turner looks forward to each class, relishing the opportunity to teach us, to shape our opinions and the way we look at the world around us.

His class is the reason I come to school.

I glance at Cameron's empty chair. School policy prohibits cell phones during class and while most people disregard that rule, I don't want to disrespect Turner. Besides, I doubt Cameron's written back in the five minutes since I checked in the stairwell.

"I've put your names in random order. Half of you will present today, the rest tomorrow. Ms…" Turner checks the slip of paper in his hand, "VanStrein. If you'll please start us off."

The lanky girl with spiky black hair who never talks to anyone strolls to the front of the room and collects her project from Turner's desk. Her face blurs as she begins, as do the rest of my classmates. A warm sheen settles over my skin, and a moment later my mouth starts to water. I don't think I'll actually throw up; bonus side effects are just part of the fun.

I keep one ear open for my name, but thankfully he's put me in tomorrow's group. Of course I don't know that until the end of class because he likes to keep us guessing. If there's anything I'd change about his teaching style, it's that. But it does force us to be prepared.

The bell rings as a guy named Tim is rambling about how long the soccer field is, and everyone stands up.

"Don't forget about the new assignment," Turner shouts over the instant chatter that erupts as soon as class is dismissed.

"You only need one photo, so you only get one week this time.
Don't wait until the last minute."

Chapter 24

It feels weird to be sneaking out in the middle of the day. Mom let me stay home but migraine or not, I can't let Amelia fail trig. One benefit to being a freak is I can help my friends—besides, I can only lay in bed waiting for Cameron to text while an elephant chews on my head for so long. Dad's napping on the couch and as much as I hate deceiving him, I'd rather he not know I'm gone than have to lie to his face.

The sun is ridiculous. My brain screams for me to hide beneath a hat and fourteen pairs of sunglasses, but that would defeat the point. I steer the car towards the Strand, doing my best to squelch the nausea that's stirring in my gut. Did I mention I get carsick, too? It's worse when I'm in the middle of a migraine.

The light turns green and I move my foot to the gas, then slam on the brakes. Two ambulances and a police car fill my review mirror, their lights stark against the blue sky. I wait until they fly past, then slowly pull through the intersection.

I don't get far.

They screech to a halt a block before the Strand—the ambulances on the shoulder on the opposite side of the street, the cop blocking oncoming traffic—and I have no choice but to stop. A car behind me honks. I twist around to flip him off but he's already pulling a u-ey. The cop looks up at the sound of squealing tires, then turns back to the reason they're all there.

Two cars—or what I assume are two cars—lie twisted against the row of trees. Metal and glass shimmer in the grass from the edge of the road to the tree line. Black tire marks start from somewhere beneath one of the ambulances and stop directly in front of where I'm parked.

My hands flutter from the steering wheel. I can't sit here. I turn off the engine and step onto the street. I glance at the cop but he's focused on the people inside the cars. Two pairs of EMTs already surround the cars, kneeling in front of the shattered windows.

I drift around my car, not wanting to intrude but unable to sit still. Suddenly I remember my camera. Turner keeps pushing us to get into the habit of carrying our cameras everywhere we go, but I'm shocked I actually remembered to put it back after downloading my last set of pictures.

I grab the camera, then hesitate. Someone could be really hurt. Dying even. Who am I to just waltz up and start taking pictures?

But this is exactly what Turner keeps talking about. Our assignment is to capture real news. I can almost hear him telling me to get over my insecurities and get to work.

My hands react before the rest of me. I take half a dozen shots before I realize I'm walking across the street. Other cars have stopped—curious moms in their fancy tracksuits, frustrated businessmen yelling into their cell phones, delivery guys grateful for a change in the daily routine—and I capture the sadness, horror, and I'd swear a hint of eagerness, on their faces. When a woman with too much makeup and a two-year old on her hip gives me a dirty look, I focus back on the accident.

A woman about Mom's age kneels over a small boy. The cop has her by the shoulders, keeping her back far enough to let the EMT work on her child. The man's hands pump up-down-up-down and I stare, transfixed, thoughts of my assignment gone.

Honking from the street snaps me out of my daze, and I lift my camera. Zoom. Click-click-click. Strong hands urging life back into a chest too tiny to endure such trauma. Tears coursing down the mother's face, mingling with blood and dirt and glass. The muscles in the cop's arms as he continues to hold her, no longer keeping her back, but comforting her as she sobs over her son.

My breathing quickens and I give my head a quick shake. The narrowed focus that takes over when I'm taking pictures stutters, and suddenly I see the other car, the other ambulance, the other horror playing out in front of me.

Two teenagers sit quietly in the grass while the EMTs poke and prod them. I had English last year with one of them. Brian. He can't tear his eyes away from the kid. His friend seems less aware of what's going on and I can't help but wonder if they were already partying this afternoon. It seems a little early, but right after school, when parents are still at work, is the easiest time to screw around.

I quietly take their picture, vowing not to let that one see the light of day. I'm not trying to get anyone in trouble, but the little voice that sometimes tells me I'm actually good at this photography thing and could even make a career out of it says that it'd be stupid not to get the entire story.

Another police car arrives, sirens blaring, and Brian stiffens. That can't be good.

One of the cops eyes me as he rushes by but doesn't question my being there so I take pictures until my battery dies.

◆ ◆ ◆

"Hey, what's your name?"

I turn around to find the cop—the one who held the mother—staring at me. "Am I in trouble?"

He looks puzzled. "Why would you be in trouble? I need your information in case we need any of your photos. You got here pretty fast and they could help with the recreation."

"Recreation?" I realize I sound like an idiot but I have no idea what he's talking about.

"For the accident investigation." He steps closer and holds out his hand. "I'm Officer Roberts."

"Biz." I shake his hand and my unease fades.

"Just Biz?"

I smile. "Yeah."

"Okay, Biz. Do you have an email or phone number where I can reach you?"

I look around, my nerves humming. No one's paying any attention to us. The ambulances have already left and the other police car is starting to pull away.

He rests his other hand on my arm.

I flinch, and he backs away.

"I didn't mean to scare you." He reaches into his pocket and pulls out a wallet, from which he retrieves a business card. "Here's my card. You can have your mom or dad call if you're not comfortable, but your photos could be a big help."

I take the card. Officer Jake Roberts. Yes, I believe what he's saying. Yes, I understand that I could help with an investigation. So why are my instincts screaming at me to get away from him?

He holds up his hands in mock surrender. "I'm one of the good guys."

I finally find my voice. "I'll have my dad call."

"That's all I'm asking." He sticks out his hand again but I just stare at it. "Drive safely, Biz."

I wait until he reaches his cruiser before heading to my car. The adrenaline from the past hour evaporates in a rush, bringing my headache back with it. I climb into the car and am just turning the key when I slam my hand against the steering wheel.

"Shit!"

The sun is setting. It's too late to flicker. Amelia failed, again.

Chapter 25

"Where'd you go?"

I freeze with one hand on the railing. So much for sneaking in quietly.

Dad's standing in the living room, arms crossed. Doing the waiting thing.

I give him the closest to the truth that I can get. "I was sick of being in my room all day so I drove around to take pictures for my next photo project."

His shoulders relax. "What's the project?"

I join him in the living room and hand him my camera. "Real news." I run upstairs to get an extra battery, then hurry back down.

He replaces the battery and the camera whirs to life in his hand. "And you already found something?"

A shudder races through me. "Yeah." My mouth goes dry. I'm not sure I can stomach looking at that scene again. At least not yet.

Dad flips through the pictures, the crease between his eyes growing deeper and his jaw dropping further with each beep of the camera.

I dig the cop's card out of my back pocket. "One of the cops asked me to call. Said they might want to use some of my pictures for the investigation." The words feel heavy, surreal. My gaze drops to the carpet. "I haven't looked through them yet so I don't know if they're any good. They probably won't be much help."

"Biz, these are really good."

"Whatever."

"No, really." He lowers to the couch but his eyes never leave mine. "They're also pretty graphic. Are you okay?"

For once, I don't mind the question. I shake my head as tears slip down my cheeks.

The camera thuds on the coffee table and his warm hand wraps around my wrist, tugging me to his side. I lean into him. No matter how frail he gets, I still feel safe when I'm next to him.

"Do you want me to call this cop?"

I nod into his shoulder. The nausea has caught up to me. And the jackhammer in my ear. "I can throw the pictures on a CD."

"Is that something I can do?"

Probably, but it'd be faster for me to do it. By the time I explained the entire process we could have sent the disc by courier pigeon. "I can do it without even looking at the files."

"Wait here." The couch shifts as he rises. With a pat on my head, he takes the card into the kitchen. I hear the phone beep as he dials, but I bury my head in the cushions before he starts to talk.

I startle awake when a cold washcloth is set on the back of my neck. The tiny hairs stand at attention, and I can't tell if it's from the cold or the eerie sensation that I'm being watched. True, it's just Dad, but it's still a creepy feeling.

Seems like I've been feeling that way more and more lately.

Thursday is a blur, but unfortunately it's school I'm blurring through. Bishop sends me to the library where I sit at the table closest to the librarian—a new woman who's busy pecking away at her ancient computer—and struggle through yesterday's test. Amelia emailed me the questions last night but they aren't proving to be very useful. For a second I contemplate flickering again, but I've already pushed myself too far.

Most times the aftershocks of my headaches involve a kind of spaciness that leaves me detached from everything around me, combined with a weird numbness all over my body that isn't so different from when I flicker. Voices sound echoey. People move around me in a blur, then slow motion, then fast again. It's all I can do to stay upright and focus on whatever's directly in front of me. I get looks, sure, but for the most part everyone knows I get killer headaches and doesn't ask about the rest.

Except for Bishop. He could give two shits that I'm sick. I flip over the test and scan the back. More of the same. I glance up and catch the librarian watching me.

"Didn't study?" she asks, a condescending sneer marring her otherwise pretty face.

Librarians are supposed to be nice. And old. Matronly. This woman acts like she's doing us a favor, when really she's just a glorified study hall monitor. "I was sick. Still am." I wipe my nose on my sleeve, then cough into my hand.

The librarian wrinkles her pert nose and turns back to the computer. "You're supposed to go back to class when you're finished, so concentrate on your test."

I roll my eyes but she's not looking. I look at the test, but the questions don't make any sense. There are numbers, and spaces for what I presume based on their size are supposed to be long answers, but I can't comprehend the questions.

Literally.

It's like I've forgotten how to read.

My heart jack-hammers and I lean back in my seat. The words swim on the page, looping and graceful, in no hurry to organize themselves so I can understand what the fuck I'm supposed to figure out.

The librarian's eyes flit my way but she continues her typing, oblivious.

"Um..."

She sighs. Rolls her eyes. "What?"

"I think I need to go to the nurse."

"You're not sure? What, the test too hard for you?"

Is she for real? "Look," I say, standing up and making the chair screech on the linoleum floor. "I get really bad headaches and something's not right. I can't—" how do I even explain what's happening? I take a step towards her but my equilibrium chooses that moment to learn the polka and I stumble forward, slamming my knees onto the floor.

She hurries around the desk and kneels at my side. "Are you okay? Do you need me to go with you?" I guess being a bitch only applies when she thinks I'm just a bad student.

I try to stand, but my legs buckle. At least I make it into my chair. "I'll be okay, I just need a minute."

She goes back to her desk and picks up the phone and is speaking in hushed tones before I register what she's doing.

"No, really. I just need a minute."

I can't say how long I'm sitting there, but it seems like only moments before the nurse is there, along with Stride Right. Really? They had to bring him? They each loop an arm around me and we shuffle to the nurse's office, the weirdest three-legged race I've ever been in. My bag appears on the floor beside me, along with the unfinished test.

Thankfully Stride Right splits the second I'm off my feet.

"I'll call your mother to have her come get you." Becky's eyes are close to mine. "Did you tell her about the other day?"

Marbles roll around inside my skull. "The other day?" Crap, I shouldn't have said that out loud. Now her eyes are all buggy and she's scribbling in my chart, which is alarmingly thick.

"Biz, how many headaches have you had this month?"

"This month?" I'm more concerned about this week. "I don't know, half a dozen." Give or take a dozen.

"Six?" She's still writing.

All this counting makes the marbles spin faster. Suddenly I'm looking at the ceiling and my head's on something squishy.

"Do you have your medication with you?" I point at my bag, entranced by a water stain on the panel next to the overhead light. "Sorry, I forgot." Becky reaches for the light switch and we fall into muted darkness.

Something else is in my bag. Something I needed to do. That I was excited about.

"What is it?"

Oh god, was I grunting out loud?

Becky hands me a paper cup of water and I down a pill. Magic pill. Pill that will stop the thumping and the spinning and the—

Darkness.

"Biz?"

I don't need to open my eyes to know who that is. "Hi, Mom."

"The nurse tells me you came in earlier this week. Why didn't you tell us it's been so bad?" The cot shifts beneath her weight and I try to slide over to make room.

"It's not that bad." I force an eye open to show her that I'm just peachy, but there's two of her. I close my eye.

"Will you please let me take you to the hospital?"

I struggle to sit up but strong arms hold me down. I open my eyes fully and Becky smiles down at me. I go limp. "I don't think it's necessary."

Mom and Becky exchange worried looks.

"Fine, I'll give you the doctor." At least that'll buy me a little time to get my game-face on. He'll poke and prod and ask his usual questions, but he doesn't have any high-tech gear in his office. Most likely he'll up my dosage and tell me to stay home for a couple days, just like he has every other time I've seen him.

A voice in the back of my head warns that I can't fool him forever.

Mom smiles. "I thought you'd say that. He has an opening in half an hour. I called on my way here."

Shit. I walked right into that.

Becky helps me swing my legs over the edge of the cot and she and Mom pull me to my feet. I wobble, but manage to grab a filing cabinet before toppling over.

Becky grips my arm. "Should I get Mr. Walker back in here?"

I shake my head. "I can make it." I glance at the clock and suddenly I remember what I was so excited about earlier. My pictures. "Do you think we can stop by Turner's class on the way to the car?"

"I think he'll excuse you from whatever you have due today," Mom says.

"I know, but I really want to show him the pictures from the accident." We shuffle into the hall and I wave my hand limply at Becky.

"Can't it wait until tomorrow?"

I give her my best are-you-kidding-me look, which loses its effect considering I can barely see straight. "You think I'll be here tomorrow after the doctor dopes me up?"

"Okay fine. But can you leave the card thingy or do you need to show them to him?"

I smile. "I can leave the card thingy."

We make our way slowly through the empty hallway. Mom brushes her knuckles against the closed door, then raps a little louder when no one answers. After a moment Turner appears in the doorway.

"Biz! We wondered where you were." He looks at my mom, then back at me. "Is everything okay?"

"I have to go to the doctor and—" I glance over his shoulder and my breath catches. Cameron's watching me, his jaw tight, shoulders tense. I didn't realize he was in school today. Man, I must really be out of it.

Mom finishes for me. "She insisted on bringing you her pictures before we leave."

I struggle with my bag. It falls to the floor with a thump, and I follow, landing gracefully on my knees, again. My camera's on the bottom. I pop out the card and hold it up for Turner. "I saw an accident last night. Well, I didn't see the accident, but I got there right after it happened. Anyway, I wanted to see what you think."

I catch Cameron's eye but I'm unable to read his expression.

Turner closes his fingers around the card. "I'll look at them tonight." He reaches for my arm and helps me to my feet, then looks back and forth between me and Mom. "I talked to that cop about the man you saw at the game and—"

"What man?" Mom grips my other arm, her fingers digging harder than she probably meant to, and I flinch.

"Just someone I've seen at a few games. He gave me the creeps and with those girls missing everyone keeps telling us to tell if we see something weird. So I did."

Turner gives a quick nod. "She did better than that. She took a picture of him. Now the police—" A chair squeals on the tile floor inside the classroom, and Turner glances over his shoulder. "The police are looking into it." He releases my arm and moves us into the hallway. "Take care of yourself, Biz. It's not the same in here without you."

Chapter 26

Mom has this red camera thing from when she was a little girl where you put a paper circle with tiny pictures into a slot, then look through these goggles and click a button to see a each new picture. The moments in between are completely black, then light shines through the film, showing a new snapshot.

That's how the rest of my day goes.

Click, we're at the doctor's office, me lying on a paper-covered bed while Mom hovers nearby.

Click, a ginormous needle is coming at me, the doctor's concerned eyes never leaving my arm.

Click, we're back in the car and I'm tugging my hat lower

and lower over my eyes. Flickering now, when I don't seem to have any control over my body, would be beyond bad.

Click, I'm in bed, an ice pack on my head and every light source banished to the closet. Even the digital clock.

Looks like I'll be here for awhile.

◆ ◆ ◆

When the fog finally lifts I tug the covers off my head and take a deep breath. The air in my room is hardly fresh, but it's better than under the covers. A sliver of light peeks between the edge of the curtain and the wall, so it's either still afternoon, or it's tomorrow. And my phone's blinking its little heart out.

I push the covers back further and roll to the floor to get my phone. It's tomorrow. There's a bunch of texts from Amelia, but I skip those when I see one from Cameron.

"You okay?"

That's it. No, 'I'm sorry I haven't talked to you in a week', or 'What have you been up to?'

"Beyond shitty. Thanks for asking."

I guess I should be happy he still cares enough to text. I didn't think my comments last week were that out of line, but a week of silence has had me wondering if he not only didn't want to date me, but didn't want to be my friend either.

I crawl to my knees and push into a sitting position, and my head nearly teeters off my neck. I remember the doctor saying something about strong side effects, and while I couldn't tell you what they are, something tells me extreme vertigo is one of them. I drag the phone into bed with me and press the speed dial for Home.

Dad answers on the second ring.

"I'm up but I can't move."

"Be right up."

Moments later he's at the door with a plate of toast and water. "I was getting worried."

"Is Mom at work?"

"She'll be home soon." He sets the tray on the floor next to my bed and sits gently next to me. At first I think he's moving slowly for my benefit, but he winces as he straightens his shirt.

"She doesn't need to miss work for me. We're fine—"

"It's almost five."

I lost a whole day?

"She told me about the man at the games." That's it. Not why didn't you tell us? Because he already knows.

"I didn't want you guys to worry."

"You mean you didn't want us to keep you from coming and going as you please."

I squirm under the covers. Dad rarely gets upset with me, and I never know quite how to behave. "That's not the only reason."

"Then why?"

"Because I didn't want to accuse some random guy of being the boogey monster when he might just be someone's dad."

He rests his hand on my arm. "You did the right thing by telling Mr. Turner, but I wish you would have told us sooner. You showed me your photos and never said a thing." He closes his eyes for a brief moment and his lips set in a firm line.

My heart clenches. He's on my side and I've made him feel like I don't trust him. "I'm sorry, Dad. I don't know why I didn't tell you."

His eyes open and he smiles. "I'm not going to ask you to promise me you will next time, at least keep me in mind."

"I will."

"Now," he pats my arm, "have you checked your email?"

My phone is still blinking in my hand. "I saw I had some messages."

"Mr. Turner called about the photos of the accident that you left with him. He emailed you last night but called when he didn't hear back this morning."

I open my email app and scroll to Turner's message.

Biz, these are phenomenal. I know the paper will publish these, but you need to send them right away. They won't be relevant in another couple days.

Dad's watching me when I close my phone.

"What did he say to you?"

A huge smile smooths away whatever pain was etched on his face. "He explained about the paper and said they were on deadline. I gave him permission to submit them on your behalf."

"You did?" Headache be damned, I launch myself into Dad's arms, willing away the loop-de-loops spiraling behind my eyes. "He said he'd call this evening once he got the paper." He glances at his watch. "Should be here any minute."

I'm stunned. No, I'm beyond stunned. I'm flabbergasted. "They're really printing my pictures? For real?"

He nods.

My pictures are actually going to be published.

Dad snuggles next to me while I nibble on the toast. I force down some water, then lean back on the pillows, waiting for the thud at the front door announcing the paper's arrival.

I stop myself from wondering aloud if they'll really be in the paper at least half a dozen times. If they aren't there… well, I'll be exactly the same as I was an hour ago. No one knows Turner submitted them, so no one would know if they were rejected.

I shudder at the word. I know it's a part of an artist's life, but I wish there was a way to skip the grunt work and land in my own studio with clients lined up around the block.

Dad elbows me. "I can hear your gears grinding."

"I'm just anxious. I gave him my entire memory card. I trust him to pick the best ones, but what if I get printed in the paper and it's some whack picture of a tire or something?"

Dad chuckles. "You took a picture of a tire?"

"Well, no. I'm just saying. I wish I'd had some kind of say in what was presented."

"I think you'll forget about that when you see them in the paper."

"You're right."

When it finally arrives Dad rushes downstairs, returning a few minutes later with the paper displayed proudly in front of him.

He was right. I did forget my worries about what photo is printed. The right half of the front page is filled with three of my photos: a large one of the EMT working on the little boy while his mother watched, horrified, and two smaller: one of the kids leaning against the car, the other a wider shot of the accident. But I'm not looking at my photos. I can't tear my eyes away from the picture in the article next to mine.

It's Cameron's sister Katie, with pigtails and a missing front tooth, smiling beneath a headline that the police have formally linked her kidnapping with the recent disappearances.

Chapter 27

I stay in bed the rest of the weekend. Amelia arrives Saturday evening with three orders of cheese fries and the latest Johnny Depp movie, and I'm grateful for the brief distraction from all the shit going on in my head. Cameron can't possibly blame me for where my pictures were printed, but he just started talking to me again.

When the movie ends Amelia gives me a hug, fills up my water glass, then lets herself out. Have I mentioned what an awesome best friend she is? She may not completely understand what I'm going through, but she supports me anyways. A pang of guilt stabs me. There has to be some way I can return the favor.

The heavy fog in my brain is descending quickly—the carb overload only a temporary fix—so I send Cameron a hello text before passing out.

With the morning light, I realize Amelia brought more than just entertainment last night and I make a half-hearted attempt to do some homework. Who knows when I'll have to retake the Trig test, but at this point I don't care. I've been slacking in my other classes and I can't fail them all.

Around dinnertime Mom knocks on my door. "Are you up to eating? Dad made mashed potatoes for you."

My fingers press the back of my skull, testing for tenderness. A slight pinprick of tension radiates from each spot I touch, but I wouldn't call it pain. At least not pain as I know it. I slowly sit up.

Mom's used to this ritual, the inch-by-inch evaluation of my body that I have to do before getting out of bed. I've fallen down the stairs more times than I care to mention because I bolted out of bed at the first sign of feeling better. She waits patiently while I turn my head from side to side.

Nothing.

"Huh, I guess I'm okay." True, it's been days since I flickered, but the empty feeling I always get after a migraine seems more pronounced, more hollow. Maybe it's more than the headache, a little voice insists. I push it away. I refuse to accept that I've been wallowing because of a boy.

My heart twinges.

Crap.

I follow Mom downstairs and join Dad at the table. He looks more worn out that usual, the lines around his face deeper than I ever remember seeing them, his lips pursed to mask the pain.

I reach across the table to touch his hand. "I guess I'm not the only one who feels like shit."

"Biz," Mom warns from near the stove.

"Well…" No wonder Mom looks so beat. Worrying about and taking care of both of us is probably not how she envisioned spending her weekend, not to mention her entire life. I twist in my seat to face her. "How are you doing? This can't be fun for you."

She sets the bowl of mashed potatoes and a chicken dish on the table and sinks into her chair in one motion. "I'll survive, but thanks."

Dad serves himself, his wary eyes giving me a warning. "We were worried about you. Your mother decided to drag you to the hospital if you didn't get up this evening." Something in his eyes tells me that he wasn't part of that plan. I don't fully understand why he's always sided with me and resisted the hospital, and until tonight I've never thought to question it, but for the first time I'm curious why he doesn't have the same fears for my safety as Mom.

"Well I'm happy to report that my headache is gone." I eye the chicken and my stomach growls. "Now I'm starving."

Mom smiles, happy her daughter is feeling like herself again, but Dad keeps a close eye on me throughout dinner. As I inhale my weight in chicken and potatoes, a small knot of uncertainty sits in the center of my gut, warning me that the side effects of this particular headache are far from over.

◆ ◆ ◆

Seems I'm not the only one happy my headache's gone.

"Biz, welcome back." Bishop hands me my half-finished test as I enter his classroom and shuffles me back into the hallway. "They're expecting you in the library."

Great. At this point I'm so far behind that I'm already worrying about the next test and I haven't even failed this one yet. The same urge to flicker seizes my body, but I wait for it to pass. I need to let my body recover.

The librarian fusses over me when I arrive, but I haven't forgotten her snotty attitude last week. My sickness—or whatever you want to call it—is not why I want people like her to be courteous to me. I sit at the table in front of her desk, but only because it's required.

It's amazing how much easier it is to take a test when you can actually read the questions. That, and the fact that I remembered enough from last week to look up the answers. I breeze through the answers in twenty minutes. The librarian isn't paying any attention to me so I waste the rest of the period pretending to struggle over the answers. With five minutes to spare I push back my chair.

"I'm finished," I announce, "so I'll take this to class."

She scribbles a hall pass for me and I return to Bishop's classroom. Heads turn when I enter. Amelia gives me a questioning look and I give her a small shrug in response. I hand Bishop my test and sit down just as the bell rings.

"Biz, please stay a moment," he says.

I smile at Amelia as she passes. "Talk to you later," we

say in unison, then laugh. I stop in front of Bishop's desk. "What's up?"

"I'm glad to see you're feeling better, but I'm worried about how much you've missed the past week or so."

My stomach sinks.

"I understand my class isn't the easiest and I'd hate for you to fall behind. I'd like you to come in during lunch tomorrow so I can help you catch up."

Ugh, really? "Do I have to?"

His frown deepens. "This isn't meant to be punishment. You're a smart girl, whether you think so or not, and I hate to see students fail because of a..." he trails off.

Now I'm getting pissed. "A what?" I cross my arms over my chest.

"An illness." He says it so matter-of-factly that I almost believe that's what he was going to say. "Tomorrow at lunch. After you eat, of course, but don't dawdle."

"Fine." I turn to leave, wondering how else my headaches can ruin my life.

I arrive at Turner's class after the bell rings. An excuse dances on the tip of my tongue but it isn't necessary because the entire class applauds when I enter the room. I look around in confusion, a warm heat spreading up my neck. Turner is at his spot in front of the board, clapping louder than anyone else, the front page of Friday's newspaper taped behind him.

Well, one side of the paper. It's folded in half to hide Katie's picture, but the end of her pigtail peeks out.

I whip around to Cameron. His hands are moving, but there's no happiness in his eyes. Only complete, utter, agonizing despair. I silently plead for forgiveness, but he isn't looking at me. His eyes haven't left the newspaper.

"There she is, the woman of the hour." Turner ushers me to my desk as the room falls silent. Like they're waiting for me to say something.

"Sorry I'm late," I mumble.

The kid behind me kicks my seat. "Don't point it out the one time he doesn't care."

Turner's still smiling at me. "When I gave this assignment I admit I hoped some of you might get your pictures published in the paper, but I never imagined one of you would make the front page!" His excitement is contagious; several whispers reach me.

"So cool."

"Lucky she was there."

"Wish my pictures were good enough."

I know everyone's happy for me and I wish I could be excited, but the one person I actually want to be happy for me is sulking on the other side of the room.

Turner points at the paper. "I'd like to highlight why these are so good. Biz incorporated several of the elements I've talked about this semester, including a few I planned to introduce this week." He gives me another smile and I lower my head. I've never handled complements well, especially not in front of the entire class. He goes on about lighting and angles and effective use of cropping, but I'm only half listening. I can't stop thinking about the overly-lit school picture of Katie smiling at the chalkboard.

I don't think Cameron's blinked since I arrived.

A couple kids pat me on the shoulder, snapping me out of my daze. I look up and can't believe Turner's face hasn't split in two yet.

"Tomorrow we'll go over your next assignment. Please leave your projects on my desk as you leave."

I catch Cameron as he hurries to the door. "Cam, wait."

He pauses but doesn't look at me.

"I'm sorry."

He seems to consider this, then continues into the hallway.

I match his pace. "Cam, I wish they were never published. To make you think about her for the entire class..." I don't want to bring up Katie, not when he's finally willing to talk to me again, but it's kind of hard to ignore her.

He turns to face me. Students stream by on either side of us. "Don't be sorry. It's awesome you got published."

"But..." I hang my head. "I wish..." I don't know how to say what I'm feeling. "I know that getting published has nothing to do with Katie, but I feel horrible for reminding you about her."

He touches my arm and the tension in his face relaxes. "Biz, it'd be impossible for anything you do to remind me of Katie. That would mean I'd stopped thinking about her in the first place."

"Oh." Talk about feeling self-absorbed.

His hand moves up my arm and slides to the side of my neck. "Thank you for worrying, but this is something I have to deal with." We stop at his locker and he hesitates. "Do you have to go to your last class?"

I've missed several days but what's the difference at this point? "No."

"Can we get out of here?"

I nod, hating myself for feeling so grateful that he wants to spend time with me, but not enough to stop me from rushing to my locker to get my coat.

Chapter 28

We're sitting in Old Berta but haven't left school yet. I'm kinda worried he'll drive by the Strand. This is the best—or worst, depending on how you look at it—time of day for me to drive through there and flickering when he's finally ready to talk is not how I plan to spend this afternoon.

"Where to?" I ask, trying to sound casual.

"The boat ramp?"

Ugh. "Sure."

He starts the car and turns out of the parking lot. You'd think someone would monitor the lot so kids don't ditch last period, but no one stops us. Cameron keeps flexing his hand against the gear-shift like he's thinking through what he wants to say.

I want to hurry him along in case I flicker, then at least I'll be prepared for whatever he needs to get off his chest, but he hems and haws until we're halfway to the Strand.

He clears his throat. "I'm not really good at this, so I'm just gonna say it." I start to panic, but then he places his hand over mine and my nerves settle. "Last week sucked. A lot. I've never gone that long without talking to you and it was like someone cut off my arm or something. I shouldn't have gotten so mad at you when you were just being honest."

"I am sorry I upset you."

"I know you are. And I'm sorry I didn't talk to you sooner. With all this crap at home, and the police calling to ask if we've remembered anything new. One cop even asked if I had anything I wanted to tell them, like I've been lying all these years." He gestures through the windshield with his hand. "It wouldn't have been so bad if I'd had you to talk to."

"You know I'm always here for you." I want to rejoice at his words, to leap across the seat and wrap my arms around him, but any relief I feel is gone the moment it sweeps through me.

We're almost to the Strand.

He squeezes my hand. "I know. That's why—" He gives me a sidelong look. "Hey, are you okay?"

No. My fingers are tingling. My toes still feel normal but it'll only be a couple seconds before—

"Biz? What's wrong?"

I cling to Cameron's hand, my mind scrambling for a way to avoid flickering. "I'm fine, I just—" What? What? Pinpricks stab my toes and I dump my bag on the floor. "Oh crap!" I double over, burying my head beneath the dashboard, pushing my things around on the floor. This has worked before, but it's hit or miss how quickly I need to react to prevent the heaviness from descending.

"What the hell are you doing?"

"I dropped my herfelator." I mumble the last word—I can only think so fast with my head between my knees. I count to ten, keeping my head down until I'm certain we're past the Strand, then slowly straighten, holding my notebook proudly in front of me.

Cameron shakes his head. "Just when I think I'm starting to understand you."

I shove the notebook back in my bag. Without thinking I ask, "What do you mean?"

He waves a hand at me. "Does this seem normal to you?"

I start to color. "I dropped my notebook."

"You weren't even holding it."

Figures he'd be all attentive and notice things like that.

"Do you really think I haven't noticed that there's something…
different about you?"

Don't panic. Different doesn't necessarily have to be a bad
thing. Lots of people try to be different, hate being part of
the crowd, blah blah. True, I'm not one of those people and
would give my left kidney to be like everyone else, but that's
beside the point.

I give him a wary look. "Different how?" I really don't want
to have this conversation but I need to know what he's thinking
so I can figure out how to deal with it.

"I don't know, things like this. Spazzing out for no reason,
like when you jerk in class. Most people do that when they fall
asleep, but you're never asleep. You just suddenly twitch out of
nowhere. Everyone wonders if maybe you've got epilepsy like
your dad but just haven't told anyone."

"People talk about me? About the—" what did he call it?
"—jerking?"

"Yeah." His mouth snaps shut, like he was about to say more but stopped.

"Tell me."

"It's nothing. Just some of the guys being stupid."

I feel like the car is closing in on me. It's getting harder to breathe. "Do you... do you make fun of me, too?" Please say no. I can't bear it if Cameron isn't the friend he thought he was. "And what about Amelia? Does she make fun of me?"

"No, but what are we supposed to say? It's not like you've ever explained it."

I know the next question before he opens his mouth and wish I could leap from the moving car to not have to hear it.

"So why do you jerk like that?"

Why didn't I ever come up with an explanation? All my hours of hiding in bed and feeling sorry for myself for being a freak and I never anticipated this conversation. I shake my head at myself, but Cameron thinks I'm telling him no.

"So that's it? I'm honest with you and you can't answer one simple question?" His jaw clenches and even though I'm freaking out and still haven't come up with an answer, I can't help but notice how even when he's pissed off, he's gorgeous.

I touch his arm, his warmth spreading through my fingertips. "I want to be honest with you, Cam. I just—" I take a deep breath.

He laughs, confusing me at the sudden change in emotion, then he faces me and I realize he's still pissed. "I guess this isn't one of your better days."

Now I'm completely lost. "My better days?"

The car slows and he takes a moment to answer. We're at the boat ramp. He parks near the water and turns off the car before adjusting in his seat so he's facing me. The water shimmers in the afternoon light, highlighting his dark eyes and the dusting of stubble on his jaw.

"Some days it seems like you already know what's going to happen, like you have some magic ball that no one else can see."

My mouth drops. Now I'm really in trouble.

"I swear it's like you even know what I'm going to say sometimes." He leans his head back on the seat, resigned that he may have to wait awhile for an answer.

Words. I need words. Now.

"But I guess today isn't one of those days."

I can't believe Cameron pieced it all together. He may not know how or why, but he's noticed things I thought I'd kept hidden from everyone—even my family. Part of me is elated that this boy sitting next to me cares enough to pay that close of attention, but the rest is in a complete state of panic that someone has figured out my secret.

My voice is barely a whisper. "You've noticed that?"

His gaze narrows on me. "I'm not an idiot."

"No, I know you're not." A sudden, terrifying thought grips me: who else has figured this out? "Have you... has anyone else noticed those things?" I still haven't answered him and he's not going to put up with this deflection for long.

"Maybe, I don't know. I haven't said anything to anyone, but that doesn't mean other kids don't talk when I'm not around." He pauses, watching me closely for my reaction. "Or the teachers."

My heart stops. The teachers can't know. I've been so careful not to—Bishop's class flits through my mind. Well, maybe not as careful as I thought.

Cameron must know he's hit a nerve because he leans forward and slides an arm around my shoulders. "I'm not trying to make you feel like a freak." Too late. "I'm just worried about you and I'm sick of not knowing what it is that makes you different."

My eyes close. I try to lose myself in the feel of his hand on the back of my neck, but when I open them again he's watching me with a look so concerned, so trusting, that I spit out words before I can change my mind. "I have this… déjà vu thing. And sometimes the situation that I'm repeating seems so vivid, it's like I've actually lived it before. Conversations, stuff like that. I can recall all of it."

"Déjà vu?"

"That's all I know what to call it."

"And that's why you jerk in class?"

This might actually work. "Yeah."

"But today is a normal day so you don't know what's going to happen?"

I shake my head.

"Is this why you get headaches?"

I nod.

"Can't they do something for you? I mean, it seems like the doctors should be able to help you somehow."

"I have pills for when I get a headache." I don't like the direction this is going.

"No, I mean for the other part."

My chest tightens. It's like the weight that never came earlier is now suffocating me. I know I can trust Cameron, but it feels wrong to be telling anyone about this, even if I'm only telling him part of it.

"They don't know."

He straightens. "What do you mean they don't know."

"I've never told anyone."

"But don't you think they could help?"

I shake my head and damn if tears don't start running down my face.

Cameron's never seen me cry—not many people have—but he does exactly what I need: he pulls me into his arms and holds me against his chest until there are no tears left.

Chapter 29

By the next day, I've pushed aside the fear that Cameron is going to tell someone my secret. Even though he only knows a small part of the truth, being able to confide that little bit has lifted a weight that I never realized held me down. I float through school, my feet barely touching the ground.

My good mood doesn't go unnoticed.

Amelia elbows me on our way to Trig. "Someone got some last night."

I laugh. "No, we just talked."

"Uh-huh. I've heard that before."

I hold up my hands and contort my fingers into a parody of

the Scout salute. "Swear to Google."

She rolls her eyes as we enter Bishop's class.

I do my best to pay attention but I'm excited for Turner's class. The fact that he said our next assignment will appeal to the artsy types means I'm definitely going to like it.

The bell rings and I'm halfway to the door when Bishop stops me.

Now what?

"Good work, Biz." He hands me my test. Eighty-seven.

"Thanks." I feel semi-proud of myself. Technically I didn't cheat since I was delirious when I saw the test so this means I actually passed on my own.

The extra good news carries me to Turner's class, where Cameron is waiting in the hall, a soft smile warming his face. I slide an arm around him and stand on tip-toe to give him a kiss. "Any idea what our next assignment is?"

"Not a clue, but I can tell you're excited."

I am, and I have to say, it feels good. So much of my life is spent dreading what's waiting for me around the next corner that I rarely stop to enjoy myself.

Cameron leads me into class and we take our seats as Turner

writes a solitary word on the chalkboard: Light.

Phantom needles prick my fingers. I flex them against the edge of the desk, hoping no one is paying attention to me. Despite my good mood, all day I've been acutely aware of every glance, every look, every whisper that seems directed my way. How closely are they watching?

I shake my head and force myself to focus.

Turner's pacing at the front of the classroom, waiting until he has our full attention. "We have a broad range of personalities in this class and I try to tailor assignments so everyone has at least one project they can get excited about. We've covered sports, real life," he nods at me, "which, to mix metaphors, Biz hit out of the park, and now we're focusing on contrasting light and dark. The subject matter is completely up to you. Your assignment is to capture the contrast, preferably in a way that highlights your subject in a manner you wouldn't notice if the lighting were consistent."

My mind is already racing through possible settings for bright light and deep shadows. If I were a masochist I'd head to the Strand and shoot the trees, but I don't want to risk another migraine this week.

Turner readies his chalk. "What places have drastic contrasts between light and shadow?"

Answers pepper from throughout the room.

"The river."

"Downtown."

"My backyard."

Everyone laughs.

"The park," I say, the scene already playing out in my mind.

Turner nods. "There's opportunity for light and shadow just about any place you go, provided there's something tall enough to cast a shadow."

Tell me about it.

◆ ◆ ◆

Dad's waiting for me on the couch when I get home.

I sit next to him but don't say anything.

He stretches his arms in front of him, bending his wrists back until the tendons strain against his pale flesh. "How are you feeling?"

I shrug. "My headache's gone."

"And that's all that was bothering you? The headache?"

I give him a sidelong glance, trying to play it cool. He's just being a concerned father, nothing more. "Yeah, pretty much. Why?"

He folds his hands behind his neck, a gesture I've rarely seen him do. It somehow makes him look younger, stronger than I'm used to seeing him. "I've noticed you flex your fingers a lot."

As a reflex my fingers start to ache, the muscles suddenly tense, the skin feeling too tight. I long to stretch them but he's watching me closely.

"Go ahead." He smiles, but not in a ha-ha-I-gotcha kind of way. No, this smile is wistful, almost sad.

I relieve the pressure in my knuckles first, popping first the left hand, then the right, then I fold them backwards in front of me, much the same way he just did. I jerk to face him, but his gaze has shifted to my feet.

"Do your toes do the same thing?"

I nod once, hoping the lack of enthusiasm speaks for how much this is not a big deal. I'm trying not to panic, but it's like he's one step ahead of me. Snippets of my conversation with Cameron run through my head, him saying that sometimes I seem to already know what he's going to say. But this is different. This is Dad.

"Always with the headaches?"

"Pretty much." I swallow hard. "How... how do you know this?" I know for a fact I've never mentioned the tingling to anyone. Maybe he really did notice like he said, but I've always been so careful.

He leans his head to one side until his neck pops. Mine longs to do the same. "Just something I've noticed."

Later in my room, I replay our conversation. He can't know the truth, there's no way, but I guess it's possible I wasn't as careful as I thought. He does spend a lot of time with me. Maybe I mess with my fingers when I'm sleeping. That's the only way this makes any sense. The only comfort I have is in his final words: that he hasn't said anything to Mom.

Chapter 30

Midway through my English class a scrawny ninth grader knocks on the door and hands the teacher a note. She looks up from her lesson plan, scans the slip of paper, and narrows her gaze at me.

Crap.

"Biz, Mr. Walker would like to see you in his office."

The class oohs and ahhs and a deep flush colors my face. I start walking towards the door when she stops me.

"I'd bring your things."

Laughter follows me out the door. I take solace in the quiet hall, but it's quickly erased by the ninth grader's sneakers squeaking ahead of me.

"What the hell did I do?" I mutter.

The kid looks over his shoulder. "They don't tell me. I'm just told what class—"

I roll my eyes. "I wasn't asking you."

He quickens his pace, hustling around the corner several yards ahead of me.

I'm tempted to keep going straight and walk out the side entrance, but considering Stride Right summoned me to his chambers, skipping now wouldn't be my smartest move. I pause in front of the classroom at the corner.

Cameron's in there.

He's concentrating on whatever he's writing, his dark head bent over the desk. I send him a silent good luck and continue towards the principal's office.

The secretary is standing at attention. "Go on in, he's waiting for you."

I falter in the doorway.

Stride Right looks up. "Please close the door and take a seat."

Oh, this can't be good.

A manila folder lies open on his desk. My permanent record? I stifle a laugh. We've always joked about whether those really exist.

He studies the papers a moment longer, then places his glasses on top of them and rubs the bridge of his nose. "I'm afraid this isn't a courtesy call." I tense, hands gripping the edge of the chair. "It's been brought to my attention that your recent tests have been… questionable."

My breath catches.

"Specifically, in Mr. Bishop's class." He shuffles the papers. "If you were just failing I'd suggest you get a tutor and send you on your way, but your scores are all over the place. That, combined with a note I received this morning that states you've been cheating, leads me to believe we've got a bigger problem on our hands."

Shit, shit, double shit. I don't move. I don't breathe. Fidgeting is a sign of lying, right? Maybe if I stay completely still he'll take it all back and I can get back to class in time to hear the rest of the lecture on dangling participles.

Stride Right's still staring at me. I don't think he's gonna take it back. "Do you have anything to say?" His watery eyes bore into mine.

I don't know where to look. I'm assuming the papers on his desk are my trig tests. How bad could it really be? "Would you believe me if I said I'm just really bad at trig?"

He flattens his palms on the sides of his desk. "I would if that's what these scores demonstrated. You were consistent the first month of the semester, but then your scores jumped from barely passing to almost an A. I'd love to give credit to Bishop for being an exceptional teacher, but I think you've had more help than that. Now," he cracks his knuckles and I have to resist the urge to follow suit. "If you tell me the truth you won't get suspended—"

"Suspended!"

"—but if you continue with the excuse that you're just lazy—"

"I never said I was lazy."

He gives me a stern look and I close my mouth. "Unless you tell me how you've been cheating, I'll have no choice but to suspend you for three days. We don't tolerate cheating in my school."

"You seem to have already made up your mind. What happened to innocent until proven guilty?"

He waves his hand over the papers. "I have all the proof I need."

I stand. "Well then, there you go." I storm out before he

says another word, leaving him and the secretary calling after me. I stalk down the hall and stop in front of Cameron's class. I'm not sure if they'll make me leave right now or at the end of the day, but I need to find out if he's the one who sold me out.

By the time the bell rings I've thought of a zillion nasty things to say, but settle on something a little less accusatory.

The smile falls from Cameron's face when he sees my scowl.

I fall in step alongside him. "Did you tell Stride Right about…" I wave my hand in front of me, not wanting to say it in the crowded hallway.

His mouth drops. "What? No. Why would I tell him?" His eyes widen and he grabs my hand. "What happened?"

I spew out the story, glancing over my shoulder in case Stride Right is lurking, ready to toss me out the front door. "I didn't really think it was you, but I can't think who else would want to bust me."

As if on cue, Double J and a couple other guys run by, elbowing kids out of their way.

My eyes narrow. "That little prick."

"Who?"

"Robbie."

My ex trails the other guys, laughing at some joke only they seem to get.

"Robbie!" I shout without thinking.

He glances over his shoulder but doesn't stop. Several heads turn to look at me.

Cameron tugs on my hand but I pull away.

"Robbie, you prick!"

Now he stops. He turns on me, fists balled at his side. "What the hell do you want?" Anger burns in his eyes and he rocks back and forth, eager for a confrontation.

I don't know why I didn't think of him right away. I'm sure there are other people who don't like me for one reason or another, but he's the only one who's into petty revenge. Rage bubbles in my chest at the sneer spread over his face. "You know what I want. What the hell'd you say to Stride Right?"

By now kids have circled around us. Cameron hovers near the edge, bouncing on the balls of his feet. I'm ninety-nine percent certain Robbie wouldn't hit me, but it's nice to have someone in my corner just in case.

"What? Did you get in trouble or something?" He laughs over his shoulder at Double J and Kirk, but they don't smile.

He scoffs, rolls his eyes at me. "Whatever. You deserve it."

"I can't believe you're such a baby. Get over yourself!" My nerve endings are humming. Every inch of my body longs to lash out at him, but I've already been suspended. I take a step towards him and the crowd oohs.

Robbie straightens so he can look down his nose at me. A sense of déjà vu—real déjà vu—sweeps over me: that's the same look he used to give me when we were about to kiss. How did I not see how mean he looks? "I need to get over myself? Who's the one—"

"Hey!" A deep voice booms from down the hall.

Bodies scatter, leaving me and Robbie fuming at each other. Cameron lingers just behind me, but the rest of our friends are gone.

"What's going on here?" Stride Right rushes towards us, arms swinging at his sides.

Robbie gestures at me. "She's pissed she got in trouble and now she's—"

"Didn't take her long to figure it out." Stride Right smiles and I nearly fall over in shock. I can't believe he outed Robbie.

Robbie's mouth drops. "You aren't supposed to tell!"

Stride Right shrugs. "You must have been the obvious suspect if she already knows. Maybe you should have considered that."

It doesn't change the fact that I'm suspended, but having Robbie called out for being a douche makes this day a teensy bit better.

Stride Right faces me.

Maybe I spoke too soon.

"You left before I could tell you that you still need to finish your classes today. Get your homework before you leave and one of your friends can bring you any other assignments." I swear a smile crosses his face. "And no more causing scenes in the middle of the hallway."

"Yessir." I give him a salute before grabbing Cameron's hand and rushing down the hall, leaving Robbie standing alone.

Chapter 31

The house is empty when I get home. There's no note on the kitchen counter and as far as I can remember, Dad didn't have an appointment. A murmur of worry darkens my already-foul mood, but they would have called my cell if something was wrong.

I head upstairs to my room, but stop halfway. As soon as they find out I'm suspended I'll be grounded for at least a week. This is my last chance to do anything.

I text Cameron. "Parents not home yet. Can you hang out?"

A minute later I'm in my car on my way to meet him at the park, my camera nestled in the passenger seat. No one needs to tell me that this is the best time of day for long exaggerated shadows. I may as well make the most of my last hours of freedom.

Cameron's leaning on the hood of Old Berta, his arms folded lightly over his chest, the same blanket tucked beneath one arm. I park next to him and ease out of the car, casually slinging my bag over my shoulder, when what I really want to do is launch over the car and tackle him.

"Lucky they weren't home yet."

A twinge of guilt doesn't let me feel very lucky. "Yeah."

He reaches his hand out to mine, and we follow a winding sidewalk to the center of the park. Once he spreads out the blanket, he sets my bag on the ground, pulls me into his arms, and gently kisses me on the lips.

Well, hello.

I'm acutely aware of every other person in the park, but this kiss is totally G-rated. His lips part and his breath warms my lips. Okay, maybe PG.

Can I get a PG-13?

Cameron lingers a moment longer before pulling back and smiling down at me. "We don't want to scare the kids."

I wave a hand at the impressionable children. "Yeah, yeah."

He snorts. "They'll go home soon enough."

As if I'm supposed to concentrate on photography now.

An hour later I've got three dozen shots of a shadow creeping its way over a wooden bench. I like the way the light bathes the bench in warmth, while the absence of light leaves the plank of wood cold, stark. When the shadow fully engulfs the bench I lower my camera and glance at Cameron.

He's focused on the tree line at the edge of the park. The tallest tree here—the one we're sitting beneath—casts a spindly shadow that stretches like it's trying to grab something in the darkness. Click-click-click.

I hadn't noticed that perspective earlier and now I'm plotting to come back another evening so I can see what he does. Copying him now would seem, I don't know, unauthentic, but maybe if I come at a different time of day I could use the shots and still have it be different from his. The trees overlap, forming a canopy that shields whatever lurks inside, and if I could capture that—

Cameron's hand on my neck startles me. "How's it going?" He's moved closer, his leg just inches from mine.

"Good, but I think I want to come back at a different time of day to see the change in perspective."

He winces. "One benefit to being suspended, right?"

"Yeah, assuming I can convince my dad to let me outta the house. This might be the last time you see me for a couple days."

He trails his fingers along the edge of my jaw and down my throat, stopping at my collar bone. "We better make good use of this time then." His lips replace his fingers and my breath catches in my throat.

I peek over his lowered head to see if anyone's watching, but most of the families have already left. Good thing too, because his lips are moving up my neck and now his warm mouth is covering mine. My pulse quickens, launching a thousand butterflies loose in my stomach. I fall back onto the blanket.

Cameron stretches out alongside me and props himself on one elbow. His eyes shimmer in the waning light. "I've missed you," he whispers, before kissing me again.

My fingers curl into the hair at the back of his neck. It seems like I've thought of nothing but this for the past week, but now that we're finally kissing, his strong body pressed close to mine, I can't stop thinking about the few people still in the park.

"Cam?" I mumble, but my words are lost. I pull back a fraction of an inch. "Cam? Do you think we could go someplace else? I feel like we're on display here."

He lifts his head and two girls sitting on the bench I was photographing giggle. "Good point." He rolls off of me and runs his hand through his hair. "Where should we go?"

I sit up next to him. My place is off-limits, and I'm guessing his is too. "Surprise me."

Once I'm seat-belted into the car I realize the downside to this plan. I reach across the gearshift and brush the back of my hand against Cameron's thigh. "You're too far away."

A mischievous smile lights up his face. "Not for long." He covers my hand with his own but removes it just as quickly to shift gears.

"I was getting worried we'd end up on YouTube if we stayed there much longer."

"I wasn't thinking about other people. To be honest, I'm still not."

Okay, we need to hurry up and get to wherever it is we're going. Speaking of which. "So where are we going?"

"I thought you had a plan."

I snort. "Me? A plan?"

"Yeah, it was a long shot." Even his smile is driving me crazy.

"I have to be home in another hour, so wherever we go can't be too far from my house."

He hits the blinker and slows to turn. "Deal."

Ten minutes later we park in front of the elementary school.

I raise an eyebrow. After the adventure at the zoo on our first date, I'm determined not to question him, but when he leads me past the building towards the playground, I can't resist. "Got a sudden urge to play on the monkey bars?" He elbows me and I giggle. Two seconds at our old school and he's already reverted to pulling my pigtails.

He grabs my hand. "Come on." We walk along the perimeter of the playground, past a row of tall lights, and stop in front of the swings. He sits in one, then loops an arm around my waist and pulls me into his lap.

This could be interesting.

He scootches further back to make room. "Ready?"

I grip the chains, nervous energy making me sit upright. "Okay."

He leans back and I squeal. After a couple leg pumps we're flying through the air.

A giggle escapes me. "I'm sorry for doubting you."

The cool air blows my hair all around, caressing my face

and trailing over his fingers. The looming darkness pulls us higher and I'm overwhelmed with the sensation of Cameron's body beneath me. His closeness makes me feel safe, even as our heads rise as high as the top of the swing-set. I slide my hands over his and lean my head back. My eyes drift shut and I give myself over to the moment.

Eventually we slow. The return to earth is no less exhilarating because he's wrapped an arm across my chest and is kissing the back of my neck. The swing stops. Before I can stand he turns me around, then pulls me to him and his mouth covers mine. He's still sitting on the swing so I'm taller than him, and the change in perspective gives me a heady rush. I dig my fingers into his hair as our tongues meet. His arms tighten around me and we press closer together.

This time I break away first and run my lips over his eyes, down the arch of his cheekbone until I find the hollow in his throat. I taste his skin and he moans softly into my hair.

"Let's get off this thing." His voice is hoarse, his lips full from our kiss. A sheen in his eyes catches the fading sun and my heart leaps into my throat.

I nod.

Taking my hand, he guides me to the plastic jungle gym in the middle of the playground. There are conveniently no lights in this part of field and shadows consume the inside of the structure. We walk around to the other side.

He tilts his head back, looking up the slide. "How the hell are we supposed to get up there?"

Two slides—one twisty, one straight—descend from either side, a fireman's pole drops from the center, and a web of ropes stretches over the broadest side.

I point at the rope. "I think we have to climb that." I grab my hands behind my back and make a big show of stretching. I touch the closest rung. It's gritty from the countless people before us. My foot sneaks onto the lowest rung and I quickly pull myself up. "I'll race you."

"Hey!"

I'm halfway up before he catches me. His hand covers mine, preventing me from climbing higher until he passes me. "Cheater!"

He laughs down at me from the landing. His head sticks out over the edge and he dangles his arms, there for me if I need it.

I don't, but I let him help me over the edge.

"What do I get for winning?"

"My eternal adoration."

He rolls to his back and I ease on top of him. He stares into my eyes and the lump in my throat returns. I still can't wrap my head around the fact that it's Cam lying here beneath me, holding me, making me feel more beautiful than I can ever remember feeling.

I touch the side of his face and marvel at how real he is. The other boys I've dated were nice to me and all, but they always seemed... detached. Maybe it was my fault. Robbie said I wouldn't let him get close to me, so maybe they were just protecting themselves. But Cam... he already knows everything there is to know about me.

More than anyone ever has.

He rolls so we're lying on our sides and strokes my temple. "What are you thinking?"

My fingers brush his chest. Suddenly I'm nervous to look at him, but I force myself to meet his eyes. His warm, dark eyes that make me want to completely lose control in the middle of the playground. "I was just thinking how nice it is that you already know me. That we know each other." His fingers trail over my neck to my shoulder and down my arm. "We don't have to go through all that bullshit of getting to know each other."

"What if there are things I still want to know about you?"

I slide my hand down his side until I find the edge of his shirt. My fingers slip inside, my cold skin making him gasp. "Sorry." I move my hand further up his shirt, relishing in the smoothness of his back, running the tips of my fingers over the bumps of his spine. "So what else do you want to know about me?"

His lips part and his head dips closer to mine. "I don't remember." He moves on top of me, erasing anything else I was going to say.

Chapter 32

As much as I want to stay here forever, I do eventually need to face my parents. My body tenses just thinking about it.

Cameron notices my shift in mood. "Do you need to go?"

"Yeah." I trace his cheekbone with my fingertip, savoring in his closeness. "I don't know if I can wait five days to see you."

"How do you know it'll be five days?"

"At the very least I'll be grounded through the weekend, and since I won't be at school until Monday…" I tick off my fingers. "Five days."

"That sucks."

"And showing up hours after dinner is not going to make

things any easier."

He sighs. "Well let's go."

We disentangle ourselves and I nod at the slide. "After you."

He scootches to the edge of the platform and in an instant disappears from sight. "All clear."

I stick my feet over the edge and my stomach leaps to my throat. Two seconds later I'm slamming into Cameron and we're on the ground in a pile of giggles. I should be freaking out right now, but being around him makes everything else seem less important.

He drives to the park and pulls into the spot next to my car. Streetlights illuminate the deserted parking lot. "I don't think you're going to make it for dinner." He walks me to the driver's door and pulls me into an embrace. "Good luck. Let me know how it goes."

I give him one last kiss. "I will."

The short drive doesn't give me enough time to come up with a plausible story. I was suspended for cheating because I've been flickering. What kind of plausible excuse is there?

They're both at the kitchen table when I go inside. "Biz?" Mom calls.

"Sorry I'm late. Cameron and I were taking pictures at the park." I enter the kitchen and try to ignore the disappointed look on Mom's face and the disapproving one on Dad's.

"A little dark for pictures, isn't it?"

Dad's not cutting me any slack.

"We're studying the contrast between light and dark. You need shadows to capture that."

"Mm-hmm."

Do they know I was suspended? I expected a full-on assault the minute I walked in the door, but they just seem peeved that I'm late. A thought suddenly occurs to me, and I look Dad in the eye. "Where were you earlier? No one was here when I got home."

He looks at Mom. I follow his gaze.

"Your father had some tests done this afternoon and it went a little longer than we expected."

My heart leaps to attention. "Why didn't you tell me? I would've gone to the hospital. You should have called." My mouth snaps shut when I realize what I've said. I should've called, too. So this is how they feel. "I'm sorry."

Dad touches my hand. His eyes are glassy, more watery than normal. "They just switched my medication. Nothing for you to get worked up over."

I need to get this over with. "Speaking of getting worked up, I have bad news." I force the words past the lump in my throat. "I got suspended."

"Suspended?" Mom shouts. "What on earth for?"

I don't want to say it. Can't they just leave it at that?

"Biz." Dad's voice is about ten thousand decibels louder than it was two seconds ago. "What the hell did you do to get suspended?"

I take a deep breath. "Stride Right accused me of cheating."

They both lean back in their chairs. Finally Dad speaks. "Did you?"

"Not exactly."

Mom expels a breath she's been holding. "What do you mean, not exactly? Either you cheated or you didn't."

I hold my hands out in front of me. "I don't know how else to explain it. Sometimes things just… click for me and I remember the answers. Other times, not so much."

Dad's head cocks to the side.

What did I say?

But Mom's not done. "How long are you suspended?"

I hang my head. "Three days."

"Three days!" She's like a parrot. "Is that why you were out so late tonight?"

This is when I hate that my parents are so involved in my life. They know in a matter of seconds that I stayed out late because I knew I'd be grounded. "Maybe."

Mom sighs again. "I don't know what to say. Go to your room so your father and I can talk about you."

"Can I at least eat?" They can't deny me sustenance!

"Take it with you."

I hurry away from the table before she changes her mind.

I text Cameron to let him know they're deciding my fate. "Doesn't look good."

Ten minutes later my fears are confirmed.

Grounded for two weeks.

Chapter 33

How bad is it to sneak out on the first day of being grounded?

Yeah, I figured as much. Instead I'll try plan number two: begging Dad to accompany me to the park with me so I can take more photos.

"It's for school. It's not like I'll be socializing with anyone. They're all in class."

"A picnic is the complete opposite of what we had in mind when we grounded you."

"Then we'll eat before we go. Whatever you want." He's caving, I can tell. Grounding is more Mom's thing.

"Fine, but only for a couple hours."

I leap at Dad and give him a hug. "Thank you!"

Following Dad into the park, I can't help but think of being here with Cameron yesterday, but when Dad lays out the blanket, I banish all thoughts of Cameron from my mind. My dad and my boyfriend need to stay in very separate mental compartments.

As we eat our sandwiches, I survey the park for differences from yesterday. The sun is almost directly above us, so while the shadows aren't as vast, they're more dense than their sprawling counterparts.

A shout from the playground makes us both turn. A little boy tumbles backwards down the slide. My reflex is to take a picture, but I've had enough of real life news.

"You did that once when you were little."

"I did?"

Dad wipes his mouth on his sleeve. "Scared the crap out of your mom, but I knew you were okay. Even lying there on the ground, you had this determined look in your eyes that said you weren't going to let some silly piece of playground equipment get the best of you."

"My eyes said that?"

"Something along those lines." He smiles. "You still have that look."

"Well, I'm not gonna let some silly slide get the best of me." Memories of making out with Cameron in the jungle gym flash through my mind. I can feel my cheeks getting warm. Maybe we should change the topic. "So I didn't get hurt?"

"Just a few bruises. But that's when your mom stopped taking you to the park. Said she couldn't handle watching you get hurt."

"So that's when you took over."

"Not that I particularly enjoy seeing you suffer, but I sometimes think I have more empathy than your mother."

Interesting he said empathy and not sympathy. We studied that in English last semester. Sympathy means you feel bad for someone. Empathy means you've been in a similar situation and understand from experience what the person is going through. I somehow doubt Dad fell backwards down a slide.

"Anyway, whatever the reason, I'm glad I've been able to spend so much time with you."

"You don't miss working?"

His smile fades. "Sure, but you can only have so many seizures at work before they gently suggest you might be better off at home. My condition may prevent me from working, but it also qualifies me for disability."

Another thing I've never noticed until now: Dad never says he has epilepsy. He says he's sick or has a condition or, my favorite, he says he gets the shakes and wiggles. I lean over and give him a hug. "I hate that you're sick, but I am glad you've always been there for me. Not many of my friends can say that."

"You believe that, right?"

"What?"

"That I'm here for you. No matter what." His eyes have regained their clarity and it's like he can see right into my soul.

I turn away before he finds out something even he can't help with.

◆ ◆ ◆

After lunch I leave Dad napping on the blanket and wander the park, my camera ready. It's a lot more crowded this time of day, mostly with moms armed with strollers, diaper bags, and tottering little kids, but the occasional gray-haired couple hobble by as well. A few people look my way when I snap their picture, but I smile and wave to convince them I'm not a child molester.

I stop in front of the bench I photographed last night.

Sunlight beats on the smooth surface, leaving the scratches and divots no place to hide.

Click-click-click.

Shadows hide between the wooden slats and in the groove that's carved along the length of the bench's frame. I sit down and tilt my head back until I'm staring at the branches high above. Oh! I sit upright. I was going to take pictures of the tree line.

I lift the lens to my eye and study the branches that seem to fold inside themselves. Small gaps here and there seem wide enough to allow a person to pass through, but for the most part it's like a fortress wall.

Click-click-click.

It may turn out that none of these are usable, but it can't hurt. I slowly scan the edge, clicking as I go.

"There you are!"

My finger continues to depress the shutter, even as I turn at Dad's voice. "You scared me."

"Sorry. When I woke up I didn't see you." He holds up my cell. "You left this in your bag."

I touch my back pocket. I hadn't realized it wasn't there.

Dad nods at the camera. "You getting anything good?"

I rise. "I think so. It's hard to tell on the display." I fall in step with him as he heads back to the blanket. "You ready to go?"

"Yeah, I think I've had enough sunshine for one day."

Chapter 34

I haven't technically been banished to my bedroom, but I'm hiding there anyway. Dad may be laid back about the whole suspension thing, but Mom isn't so understanding. Better I play the role of good daughter and do the homework Amelia emailed to me.

Shortly after dinner I download the photos from the park. The ones from yesterday with people in them are pretty boring, but the time lapse of the bench turned out better than I expected. The camera didn't stay as still as it would have if I had a tripod—something else to ask for on my birthday—but the slight shift gives the montage a stop-action feel, something I'll definitely try to repeat again.

The photos jump from the edge of the park at dusk to bright sunlight. The difference is startling, even on the computer screen. The sun bleached the color from everything it touched, while the shadows seem over-saturated, luring me closer.

I flip ahead, curious to see the park's edge in the brighter light.

Leaves and branches twine around each other much like I remember, but a splash of color at the edge of the frame surprises me. I don't recall seeing anyone there. I click to the next picture and an out-of-focus little girl in a red sweater stands in my picture. How did I miss her?

Then I remember. Dad startled me and I took the last few pictures without looking. I click ahead and my stomach drops. There's a man standing behind the little girl.

Don't be stupid, I scold myself. It's probably her dad.

He's wearing some kind of blue jacket and tan pants. The photo's too blurry to see his face, but the way he holds his shoulders—hunched forward like he bends over a lot—makes the hair on the back of my neck stand up. I can't tell if it's the same man from the games but something about the way he's standing feels familiar.

Time for a break. I push away from my desk and head

downstairs to get a drink of water. The evening news drifts into the kitchen. "…last seen wearing a red sweater. Police say—"

The glass slips from my hand, shattering at my feet.

"Biz? What happened?" Mom's at my side in a matter of seconds, picking the largest shards from the floor.

"The TV." My mouth is so dry I can barely get the words out. "Is another kid missing?"

Her eyes water as she looks up at me. "Today at the park."

My head jerks in the direction of the living room.

"Dad said you two were there today. Can you imagine if you'd been there when it happened? How horrible for—"

"I… I think I saw her."

Dad twists around on the couch. "You did?"

I point at the ceiling. "I have her picture."

Mom and Dad follow me up the stairs. We crowd around my computer and stare at the picture filling the screen.

Mom covers her mouth with her hand. "You're sure you took this today?"

I look at Dad. "This was the last one I took before we left. I wasn't looking because you surprised me, so I didn't know what I'd taken until just now."

"We have to call the police," Mom says. "This could be the first picture they've had." She rushes from the room and her footsteps fade down the stairs.

My breath is coming too quickly. My heartbeat is all over the place. I might be able to help, but I'm also freaking out to once again be involved in an actual life or death situation.

Dad rests his hand on my shoulder. "You could help stop this kidnapper."

My insides turn to liquid. It's time to stop hiding behind my fear of being different. This is about more than just me. I could actually save this little girl and I need to start by telling Dad the truth. I force a deep breath, digging deep for the courage to tell what I've never told a soul. "I think I can help her."

He tilts his head and gives me a puzzled look. "That's what we're talking about."

"No, help her…" my voice is so low I can barely hear it. "Like stop her from getting kidnapped."

Dad straightens.

And I lose my nerve.

He moves to my bed and sits down. "Can I ask you a question?"

"I think you just did."

His eyebrows raise.

"Sorry."

He looks down at his hands hanging loosely between his knees. "What happens after your fingers and toes start to tingle?" My mouth drops as he meets my gaze.

"You know? How do you know?"

His fingers stretch, as if by reflex. "It used to happen to me."

We stare at each other for what seems like hours. A thousand questions tumble over themselves in my mind, all fighting to be the first to fly off my tongue.

"Used to? You mean you can't anymore?" It never occurred to me that this might someday go away.

He shakes his head. "How long has it been happening?"

"Since I was thirteen. The first time it happened was right after my first visit to the orthodontist. I had that nasty mold in my mouth twice!"

A sad smile dances on his lips. "Mine was after I broke my arm when I was fourteen. The doctor reset it without anesthesia. I've always wondered if traumatic events trigger the syndrome. If I remember correctly, you were terrified to get braces."

My tongue slides over my straight teeth. "It didn't turn out so bad."

He leans forward on the bed. "So how far back do you go?"

"About eighteen hours."

"And how often does it happen?" He raises a finger in thought. "Is that why you were so sick last week?"

I nod. "If I flicker two days in a row it's really bad. Remember when I went to the ER last year? I was trying to fix a test and—" I snap my mouth shut. Crap. True confessions wasn't part of the plan.

He shakes his head. "I figured as much. I did the same thing in school."

Relief washes through me. I'm not the only evil manipulator in the family.

"So eighteen hours." He falls silent as he does the math.

"I'd have to leave at dawn. And that might not be enough time."

"This is a bad idea. We don't know who that man is. You could get hurt."

"It's not like I'm gonna walk up to the guy. I haven't thought it through yet, but I figure I'll find the girl and make sure she's safe." I take a breath. "Dad, for the first time in my life I have the chance to truly help someone. And not just help them with something stupid that won't matter in five years," I think of Amelia and our tests, "but I can change someone's life. Who knows what that girl has already gone through tonight."

I don't need to say more. The pain in his eyes says enough. He's going to let me do it.

I change the subject before he protests any more. "So when did it stop?"

"The last time I—what do you call it? Flickering? The last time was the night you were born. The joy I felt watching you come into the world... I can't describe it." His face gets a faraway look and he stares over my shoulder. "You were so beautiful, so perfect. Of course the first thing I wanted to do was repeat the whole night.

"But in addition to watching you be born a second time, I also hoped I could make things a little easier on your mom. The delivery was hard for her and I thought if I got her to the hospital a little sooner, maybe massaged her back during the contractions, that I could make it better for her.

"You were born around sunset so I had to wait until morning

to flicker. I made up some excuse to your mom for why I needed to leave, then drove out to the Sticks to—"

I interrupt. "The Sticks?"

"This stretch of trees over by the river. The light was always perfect there."

I grin. "I call it the Strand."

"Huh." He smiles back at me. "What do you know?"

"So you flickered that morning?"

"I tried to. For a reason I still don't understand, the light affected me differently that day. Instead of flickering, my body started convulsing and I crashed head-on into a car in the oncoming lane. Nearly killed myself and the other driver."

This is news to me. "Why didn't you tell me?"

He rubs the back of his neck. "Those first few days were such a blur, neither of us wanted to talk about it afterwards. I was in the hospital for weeks after you and Mom came home and she had to take care of you by herself. Once I was released we thought we'd pick up where we left off, but I've never been the same."

"The epilepsy?"

"That's what the doctors labeled it, but they don't know what it is. Of course I've never told them the most important part." He shrugs. "Who knows what they'd find inside my skull if they ever cracked me open. For now I collect my disability and live life as an invalid."

I can't imagine waking up one day and having your entire life taken away. To be given a label that makes people feel sorry for you, when really you're a modern miracle.

Funny I've never thought of myself that way.

"Does Mom know?"

"No. She's wondered, I'm sure, especially before you were born and I flickered all the time. But she's never asked many questions."

"And now I'm repeating what you went through."

"It seems so. And that's why I hate for you to flicker even one more time. There's no telling what could be the trigger for you. If trauma makes it start, maybe extreme joy makes it end. Knowing you've saved a girl's life could be enough to push you to the edge."

He's right. I know he's right. "I still have to do it."

He rises and stops in front of me. Wraps his arms around me. "I know."

Chapter 35

"Yeah I'll pick you up, but how are you gonna get out of the house?" Cameron asks.

"If I leave early enough they won't realize I'm gone." Dad agreed to check on me in the morning so Mom will think I'm here, but I'm not ready to tell that to Cameron yet. "So you'll be here at five?"

He groans. "Why so early?"

"I'll explain then." A benefit to always being a little weird is Cameron stopped questioning some of my stranger requests a long time ago. "See you in the morning."

"Good night."

Mom knocks on my door a few minutes later. "The police want your camera card thingy."

I sit up. "I can't just email them the picture?"

"I asked. They said they need the original card to verify it's not doctored."

"Why would I? Never mind." If it helps the little girl, I'll do it. I roll off the bed and grab my camera off the desk. I pop out the card and hand it to Mom. "Good thing I didn't erase it when I downloaded them earlier."

Mom cradles the card in her hand. "I'm so proud of you. It makes me happy to see you doing something you love, not to mention something that's helping others." She gives me a quick hug then heads back downstairs.

I know I should sleep but I spend hours studying the pictures, memorizing every detail so I won't have any doubt where to find the little girl. I can tell you the color shirt on each boy on the swings, the sandbox to grass ratio of toys, and how many strollers are lined up near the picnic tables. There's a soccer ball in the edge of the frame, and I presume that's what drew the girl to that spot in the first place. The only thing I still don't know is the man's face.

My alarm goes off a couple hours later, followed by a text from

Cameron that he's parked around the corner. I arrange my pillows under the blankets, then roll my eye at my ridiculousness. This isn't a made-for-TV movie. I shove the pillows to the floor then slip outside as quietly as I can.

My stomach drops.

It's raining.

Not only that, a thick blanket of clouds separates me from the stars, and in another hour it'll separate me from the sun as well.

How is this gonna work?

Cameron flashes his lights and I hurry to his car. I have to follow the plan and hope the clouds break in time.

◆ ◆ ◆

Cameron leans across the seat and kisses me. "I didn't expect to see you until Monday."

I force a smile. "Something's come up."

"Are you going to tell me the big secret?"

"Yeah, but not here. Can we go to the boat ramp?" We could go someplace closer, but the boat ramp is only a few minutes from the Strand.

"Sure." He pulls away from the curb. Neither of us is awake so the only sound is the gentle thwmp-thwmp of the windshield wipers as they push away the rain. Because I don't have much time, I've decided to just spit out the facts and hope Cameron accepts it fast enough to help. It might have been smarter not to involve him, to just drive there myself like I always have, but he deserves the chance to help his sister.

He parks in what I've come to think of as 'our spot' and shifts in his seat to face me. "I'm dying here. Spill it."

I take a deep breath and look into his eyes, then quickly lower my gaze. What if this doesn't work? What if he thinks I'm a nutcase and won't do it? Then my inner voice speaks up: What if he does believe you and it does work and you've given him a way to redeem the guilt he's carried for the past four years? Because I finally see that's what's been going on. He can't let go of Katie because he thinks it's his fault she disappeared.

"I think I can help Katie."

He pulls back, his eyes wide. "What?"

Okay, that wasn't the best way to start. "Yesterday I went to the park with my dad to take pictures for Turner's class and I somehow photographed a little girl right before she got kidnapped."

His mouth drops. "The one yesterday?"

I nod.

"How? Did you tell the police? And why did we have to drive all the way out here for you to tell me?"

"We gave the pictures to the police last night and they've already started doing their thing, but I can do more." I pause. I've had eight hours to think about this and I still don't know how to tell him. A flash of lightning strikes in the distance, sending ripples of panic down my spine. What if the rain doesn't clear?

He slips his fingers through mine. His dark eyes are so concerned, so understanding, that for a second I forget why we're here. "How?"

I clear my throat. "You know my déjà vu thing?" He nods. "Well it's a little more complicated than what I told you." And I tell him everything. About the first time at the orthodontist, cheating on tests, repeating the first time we kissed. About how I help Amelia with homework and how I wished more than anything I could have done something to help Katie when she disappeared. His eyes don't leave mine the entire time I'm talking, and he's still staring even when I've finished.

"Worst of all, I repeated the day the second girl was taken

and it didn't occur to me that I could help her until it was too late." I squeeze his hands. "I'm not making that mistake again. I know exactly where this girl was when she was taken."

Cameron's eyes are still frozen on mine, but he finally closes his mouth. Swallows. His voice comes out a whisper. "So you can actually go back in time? And change stuff?"

"Yeah. For the first time I've realized I can use this ability—" because I now understand this is more than just a condition, "—to help someone other than myself. I can actually save someone's life."

"But is it dangerous for you?"

I hesitate, but he's too overwhelmed by everything I've told him to notice. "No. I'll get a headache, but I'm used to that."

He closes his eyes. "I don't get why you're telling me all this right now. If you're going to—what did you call it? Flicker? If you're gonna flicker, why do you need me?"

A lump jams my throat and I struggle to swallow. "Because if this is the same man who took Katie, this could be your chance to help find out what happened to her."

His lips part but he doesn't speak. Doesn't breathe. A tear slips down his cheek and lands on the back of my hand, but instead of wiping his face he turns to look across the river.

Hints of orange color the treetops but rain still pounds the windshield, drums the metal roof.

I trace my thumb along the path of the tear.

He looks back at me. "What do I need to do?"

"Drive me to the Strand."

"The Strand?"

A laugh escapes before I can catch it. "You know that stretch of road not far from here where the trees stand taller and straighter than anywhere else for miles?"

He cocks his head.

"Okay, maybe I'm the only one who notices things like that." I try again. "The place where I dumped my books on the floor and freaked out."

He nods. "What's so special about that place?"

"Because the trees are so tall and grow right alongside the road, I can flicker pretty much any time of day. The other day I was trying not to flicker. Sticking my head under the dashboard was the only way to get away from the light."

A smile tugs at his lips. "I thought you'd lost your shit."

"It was the first thing I thought of."

"But this time you want to flicker."

"More than anything."

We stare at each other a heartbeat longer, then he starts the car. "Let's go."

"There's just one problem."

"What's that?"

I point at the sky and the maddening absence of sunlight.

He follows my gaze. "You can't flicker in the rain?"

The lump in my throat returns. This isn't going to work. "No."

He leans forward and peers at the sky as if the determination in his gaze can make the clouds disappear. "Is the Strand the only place you can do it?"

I shake my head.

"What if we drive away from the storm? It can't go forever, right?"

Relief floods through me. I was so focused on how this would help Cameron that it didn't occur to me that he might help me. I pull out my phone and in seconds the satellite image of the storm appears.

He points at the display. "It looks like it's clearing up to the west. Let's drive until the rain stops." He looks up from the phone, his face inches from mine. "Will that work?"

I press my forehead to his. "It has to."

Five minutes later, he glances at me as we drive past the Strand.

I shake my head.

"It was worth a shot." We continue west, eyes glued to the horizon.

I can't stop checking my watch.

Cam notices after the fifth time. "What does the time have to do with it?"

"I go back roughly eighteen hours, but it's never exact. I took that picture around one o'clock and it's…" I check my watch again, "… six thirty now. If I don't flicker soon, she'll already be gone."

The car lurches forward and I grip the seat.

Cameron stares straight ahead. The trees whip by. And like a miracle, a streak of sunlight bursts through the clouds.

I grab Cameron's hand and squeeze.

The trees grow denser and my heart lifts. This might work.

"Does it matter how fast I go?"

"No, but the longer we're in the flickering light, the better."

Sunlight pulses across the dashboard.

Light. Dark. Light. Dark.

My eyes stutter and my heart jumps around in my chest, but this time I don't I blink it away. My fingers start to tingle, then my toes. "It's working."

He looks at me, eyes wide.

"You won't be able to see anything. I don't even think you'll realize I'm gone. But it's happening." I sink into the seat, then I'm skyrocketed up and—

Chapter 36

I'm sitting on the blanket in the park.

Dad's next to me and we're surrounded by the remains of our lunch.

"I'm gonna wander around and take some pictures on the other side of the park." I leave him sitting there and head towards the edge of the woods. It's impossible to tell how much time I have, or if I'm too late. All I can do is try to find the girl.

Red sweater, red sweater. I scan the children on the playground but no red stands out. The toys are still in the sandbox, and the boy in the orange sweatshirt is on the swings like he's supposed to be. There's one less stroller near the benches, but I don't know if that's good or bad. Please please please let me not be late.

I round the playground and—There!—a flash of red catches my eye. Near a clump of trees, on the opposite end of the park from where I'd been sitting with Dad. I let out a breath I didn't realize I'd been holding. The little girl is running circles around her mother, who's sitting on the blanket and holding out a snack of some sort. No one's taken her; she's safe.

I need to keep it that way.

I double back, but instead of returning to my blanket, I head for the tree line. I check my distance from Dad and the playground. This is the spot in the picture. The small break in the trees is a couple feet away, and the soccer ball is at my feet. How long did it sit here? With a park full of kids, I can't imagine a soccer ball would be forgotten very long. I turn away from the trees to face the crowd and a man is standing directly in front of me.

"Hi Biz."

I take a step back and gasp. "Mr. Turner, you scared me."

He nods at my camera slung over my shoulder. "I'm glad you're using this time to your advantage."

I appreciate him not reprimanding me for being suspended.

Any other teacher and I wouldn't care, but Turner's opinion is important to me. But something feels off. "What are you doing here?"

"I was intrigued by your comment in class yesterday. About the light and shadows at the park." As if on cue, the branches overhead shift in a slight breeze and a flash of sunlight streaks across his face. He smiles and a chill runs down my back as a realization strikes me: he's wearing a blue windbreaker and tan pants.

I take a small step back. "Why aren't you at school?" It can't be him. It has to be a coincidence.

He ignores my question. "You've always been my favorite student."

My breath catches. His words—the same as at the football game—no longer sound like a compliment.

"You know, my daughter Jessica was only a couple years younger than you when she disappeared, but she didn't behave like you do. The cops say she ran off but..." he shakes his head and takes a step closer.

I look over his shoulder. No one's paying attention to us. I have a clear line of sight to the main part of the park, and I spot the little girl sitting next to her mom. She's still safe. If I can talk to Turner long enough maybe they'll leave and this will actually work.

My focus returns to Turner. My teacher. He's moved closer, only arm-distance away. My gaze flits to Dad, still sitting on the blanket. "My dad's probably wondering where I am. Still grounded, you know." I lift my shoulders and force what I hope sounds like a casual laugh.

"He can't hear you from here."

Alarm bells clang in my head. My pulse skyrockets. I step to the side, trying to put some distance between us, but he moves with me.

"I wish you hadn't paid so much attention to those girls."

"What?"

My camera slides off my shoulder and I lurch to the side, but his strong hand clamps onto my wrist.

"Don't fight it, Biz. It's easier if you don't fight."

A sickly sweet odor wafts over me. I jerk my arm as hard as I can, but his hand is like a vice. I open my mouth to scream but a damp cloth covers my face before I can make a sound. My grip loosens on my camera as I slip to the ground and into darkness.

◆ ◆ ◆

I'm moving. I'm barely conscious and lying on my side on something cold and hard. It feels like there's sand inside my head.

Music plays not far from me. I open my eyes and a fresh ripple of fear grips my stomach. I can't see anything.

Well that's not true. Faint light trickles past the edges of whatever's tied around my head. I reach to pull it off but my hands don't budge. I wiggle my fingers. My arms are tied behind my back.

My chest tightens.

Stop. Take a deep breath. I can't panic now. I roll onto my stomach and moan.

"Are you awake?"

Turner. He took me. He kidnapped me. My chest convulses. Why didn't I tell Dad what was going on? I'm such an idiot. It never occurred to me that the man from the picture might change his actions—I thought I'd have to stop him from taking the girl. My being there must have kept her away, so when he got here—

The vehicle stops suddenly and I'm thrown across the metal floor. More light sneaks beneath the blindfold and I can see the ridged surface of the-is this a van? How did he get me here without anyone seeing? I try to remember the place we were standing. Maybe that gap in the trees led to a path.

"We're almost there."

Almost where? I have to do something.

I roll over and the light changes. It's not as strong.

I roll back. Definitely brighter facing this way. There must be a window just above me.

The fear ebbs ever so slightly, pushed away by a determination so strong it nearly lifts me off the floor. If I can get this stupid thing off my head, maybe there's enough light...

I press the side of my head against the floor, feeling for a groove. The cold metal bites into my cheek. I drag my face against the edge but it doesn't catch the blindfold. The metal is too smooth.

I roll until I bump into something harder, sharper. I shove my face against it and gasp as it slices into my flesh. Heat washes down my face but I don't pull away. Whatever cut me is caught on the blindfold. I slowly pull down, slipping the cloth off my eyes and onto my forehead.

I flop back over, toward the light.

"Hey! What are you doing back there?"

I open my eyes. The light blinds me, seeming even brighter after not being able to see. The flicker isn't strong, but it has to be enough. I stare at the light, welcoming the fangs that leap from the sun, through my corneas, and into my skull. My vision blurs when my fingers start to tingle, a mixture of tears and blood coloring everything a light pink.

The van slows but I've already started. My toes tingle and I hold my breath, waiting for the heaviness to weigh me down.

A hand grabs me. "How'd you get that off your face? You shouldn't be awake yet!"

I close my eyes. I'm turned away from him but I don't know if he can see my face and maybe he'll think I'm unconscious again.

The van comes to a stop.

The tingling fades.

Rough hands turn me onto my back, shake me. My mind refuses to connect this monster with the man I trust.

I go limp.

"Are you awake?" He shakes me again.

His breath overwhelms me, a disgusting mixture of whiskey and onions that tickles my nose. Is this what the other girls faced? I fight the urge to sneeze, hoping he doesn't notice I'm holding my breath.

He lets go of my shoulders and I'm slowly letting out my breath when he slaps my face. It takes every ounce of strength not to react. Needles stab my cheekbone where I cut myself. A warmth slides over my chin and drips onto my shoulder.

But I still don't move.

Moments later we start moving again. Despite everything that's happening, a small glimmer of hope lights inside my chest. He didn't put the blindfold back on.

I don't dare open my eyes until the light flickers through my eyelids. The tingling starts quickly, sweeping from my fingers to my toes. If I could hold my eyes open with my fingers, I would, but instead I fight my instincts and stare at the window until the crushing weight slams me into the floor.

Just a couple seconds longer.

Finally, finally, the heaviness lifts and I'm rising up, up, up and—

I'm in the jungle gym, pressed against Cameron, his tongue sliding against mine.

I pull back quickly.

He traces his hand along my cheek, then jerks back. "What the hell? Why are you bleeding?"

"Um… I think I hit my head on the side of the… the thing…" There's nothing sharp up here. It's a kids' jungle gym.

He pulls me into a sitting position and cradles my face in his hands. There's a streak of blood on his nose. "It's bleeding pretty bad. I should take you home."

"Yeah. That's probably a good idea." I've flickered into a lot of weird situations, but this is the first time I've gone from being tied up in the back of a kidnapper's van to kissing my boyfriend. And the first time I've brought an injury with me. The tears start before I can stop them.

Cameron presses his sleeve to the cut. "Hey, what's wrong? There's something more than just this."

Turner's betrayal nearly crushes me. How do I being to explain? "I guess I'm just a little overwhelmed with everything. You, being suspended…"

He kisses my forehead and pulls me close. "I can take you home if that's what you want."

I nod into his chest, grateful for this brief moment of calm. Because as soon as I get home all hell's going to break loose.

Chapter 37

I get home earlier than I did last time, so Mom and Dad are just sitting down to dinner and aren't pissed off at me for being late. I'm so freaked out by everything that's happened in the past couple hours that I forget what I look like.

Mom leaps from the table. "Oh my God! Biz, what happened?"

I touch the gash. It's stopped bleeding but dried blood crusts the side of my face. "I hit it on…" I trail off, hoping she won't notice.

Dad also hurries to my side, but the expression on his face isn't wild and panicked like Mom's. It's calm and determined.

Experienced. He studies me as if he knows something more is going on but isn't about to ask right now.

Mom whirls into action, soaking a towel in the sink and cleaning my face. "This is deep. I know you hate the hospital, but I think this needs stitches."

"Can't you just put a bandage on it? I just want to lie down."

She peers closely into my eyes. "My instincts tell me that's the last thing I should let you do, but I'm going to trust that you'll tell me if you start to feel worse. And I fully intend to check on you every half hour."

"Deal." I catch Dad's eye as Mom steps back and give him a small nod. I don't know what I'm expecting, but I get the feeling he already knows, even though I'm not supposed to tell him until tomorrow.

He follows me up the stairs and closes the door behind us. "What really happened?"

"Dad, I need to tell you something."

He sits on the bed, folds his hands in his lap.

"You aren't supposed to know this until tomorrow but I need your help."

He cocks his head but doesn't interrupt.

"I know about you, about how you flicker. I do, too." He takes a sharp breath. "I know that you already suspect it. I'm repeating right now, and tomorrow we talk about this. I normally try to keep things as close to how they happened, but I'm in a lot of trouble."

"What happened to your head?" His words are slow, deliberate.

"Tomorrow when we're at the park I accidentally take a picture of the kidnapper."

"Was it the man from your other pictures?"

I shake my head and a jolt of pain shoots down my neck. "I don't realize I have the pictures until I get home—that's when I tell you—and so I went back to try to stop him. But things got screwed up and he took me instead."

Dad leans forward, his mouth set in a firm line. "Did he hurt you?"

He doesn't need to know the man hit me. "I did this trying to get my blindfold off. I flickered again from inside the van. That's how I'm here now."

The color drains from his face. "You flickered inside a flicker?"

My heart stutters. "Yes." If he hadn't reacted that way I'd be able to handle this, but now I'm heading into a full-blown panic attack. "We need to tell the police. I don't know how to explain without telling them the full story, but we have to stop him." I hesitate and Dad leans closer.

"There's something more."

"I know the kidnapper."

"What do you mean you know him?"

The ache in my chest strengthens. A sob escapes my throat. "It's Turner."

His shoulders slump. "All this time?"

"I didn't stick around long enough to ask. But I got the impression he's done this before." A phantom pain grips my wrists where they were bound. "Do you really think he took all those girls? Even Katie?"

Dad rises from my bed and engulfs me in his arms. "I don't know. We need to figure out a way to tell the police without exposing you." I nestle my head into the safety of his chest. He may not be as strong as other men but his unfaltering love more than makes up for anything he may lack. "I'm so proud of you. I'm terrified of what's going to happen when you catch up to your present, but I'm not going to let your sacrifice be for nothing."

My sacrifice? What the hell does that mean? I pull back and level my gaze at him. "What don't I know?"

He shakes his head slowly. "I don't know for sure, but the trauma you're putting on yourself could be more than your brain can handle. This goes beyond a simple headache. I'll have to make sure you're at the hospital in time."

Once I get past being thoroughly freaked out, Dad and I come up with a plan. He calls the police and tells them he's noticed someone loitering near the park around lunchtime, when all the little kids are there, and that maybe they should check it out tomorrow. At first they don't want to listen to him, but they have so few leads that they finally agree. I worry we're not acting fast enough, but if there's any chance those girls are still alive they need to surprise Turner.

And the waiting begins. My anxiety is so strong it's like another person in the room, and the courage that got me to this point evaporates, leaving me a quivering mess, hiding beneath the covers.

I debate calling Cameron, but he's already done his part. If this doesn't work and they don't catch the guy... I couldn't bear for him to know. Better he be surprised like everyone else. Assuming everything goes the way it's supposed to and I don't end up a vegetable, or dead, I'll tell him everything afterwards.

Dad tells Mom that he'll check on me and we spend the evening swapping stories about the stunts we've pulled when flickering. He was more of a trouble-maker than I am, deliberately pulling pranks on teachers and getting suspended every couple months.

"You?" I ask, shocked.

He shrugs, a sly smile brightening his face. "Not everyone uses their super powers for good."

"Speaking of being suspended…"

He quirks a brow. "You?" he mimics.

"They think I'm cheating. Which I guess technically I am, but it's not like I'm stealing tests or sneaking answers into the classroom. I still have to memorize what's on it."

He chuckles softly, a deep throaty sound I haven't heard since I was a little girl.

My eyes flutter closed.

"How long have you been awake?"

I quickly do the math. Saturday morning, about an hour yesterday, and about an hour now. "Not long enough to be this tired. I didn't get much sleep Friday night, but I'm not usually this exhausted." I can barely keep my eyes open. And forget lifting my head. Even forming words is getting difficult.

"The double flicker might have different effects. You should sleep and let your body catch up." He pauses. "What time did you leave the van?"

"I don't know for sure. Maybe one o'clock."

"If they catch this guy things might get a little crazy since we gave the tip, but do not wait to take your pills."

I nod obediently, grateful to finally have someone who understands.

"I think you should take one now."

"But the doctor says I shouldn't take one if I don't have symptoms."

The corners of his mouth droop and the humor vanishes from his eyes. "If it gets as bad as I think it will, an extra dose of medicine is going to be the least of your problems."

Chapter 38

I might actually die.

Those four words are stuck on repeat in my head.

I might never see Cameron again. Or Amelia. Or even Stride Right.

What will my parents do? Will Dad tell Mom the truth?

Will everyone know, or will they think I died from some freak explosion in my brain?

Or what if I don't die and I end up a vegetable in one of those nursing homes, where people visit every other Tuesday and sit around uncomfortable, not sure if I can hear them and wondering how long they need to visit the girl who hasn't moved or spoken or even blinked in years.

That would be worse than death.

I took my pill hours ago and Dad left me alone in the darkened room, but as tired as I am, I can't sleep. This could be the last time I have coherent thoughts. The last time I'm able to express myself. Why am I hiding in my room?

I call Cameron.

"Hello?" His sleepy voice reminds me that it's the middle of the night.

"Oh crap, sorry. I didn't realize how late it is."

"Biz? What's up?" He clears his throat and I can picture him running his hand through his tousled hair.

"I couldn't sleep and wanted to hear your voice."

"Did your parents freak out?"

That seems so long ago. "The blood scared my mom, but Dad convinced her to let me just sleep."

He doesn't answer.

"Cam?"

"Hmm?" He yawns. "Sorry. I'm really tired."

Disappointment stings my heart. "It's okay, go back to sleep."

"You sure?"

"Yeah, we can talk tomorrow." My heart aches, but it's not his fault. He doesn't have a clue what's going on and I made the decision not to tell him. I give up my plan to call Amelia. It would just be the same thing.

I have to do this alone.

Well maybe not entirely alone. When I wake up, Dad's at the foot of my bed, reading a book. Sunlight streams through the open window.

He sets down the book when he sees I'm awake. "How are you feeling?"

"So far so good. But I couldn't sleep."

He smiles, a sad expression that worsens the ache in my chest.

I look at the window again. "What time is it?"

"Almost eleven."

I bolt upright. I've slept away half of what could be my last day. I need to talk to people, to do things, to—

Dad puts his hand on my foot. "Calm down."

"I didn't say anything."

"I can see it in your eyes. I didn't mean to scare you last night, I just wanted to make you aware of the dangers. You might have a headache like any other time and no one will be the wiser."

I look away. "It's a little late to unring that bell."

He sighs. "I know, and I'm sorry."

We sit like that for awhile. I'm grateful to have him here, to spend time with the one person who doesn't need me to explain.

At noon I take another pill and bury beneath the covers.

At one o'clock the ice picks begin.

◆ ◆ ◆

I'd like to say I sat on the edge of my bed while the police tried to catch the man, but the next thing I know I'm waking up in a brightly lit room, surrounded by beeping machines and bags full of clear fluid.

For once the light doesn't cause me pain, but I close my eyes anyway. My fingers are tingling, but it's a different feeling than what I've grown used to. Rather than beginning at my fingertips and working its way up my hands, this is more focalized, and, come to think of it, only in one hand.

I lift my head. My hand lies motionless next to my hip, a clear tube protruding from a bandage in the center of my hand and snaking to one of the bags suspended over my head.

This can't be good.

The door opens and Cameron enters, eyes downcast. He's halfway to the bed before he looks at me. A smile lights up his face. "You're awake!"

"How long have I been asleep?"

He pulls a chair close to the bed and covers my free hand with his. "They've had you out for a couple days. Said you needed time to recover after the surgery."

"Surgery! What'd they do to me?"

Cameron pulls back slightly, a look on his face like he realizes he said something he wasn't supposed to.

"Cam, tell me."

"They had to operate. Your dad brought you here Saturday afternoon and they found a mass in your brain. They said if they didn't remove it you could die."

They operated? On my brain? Does this mean they know? A machine near my head starts beeping and we both stare at it, transfixed. With all these tubes and wires it's hard to tell what goes to what, but I'm pretty sure that machine says I'm completely freaking out.

"I probably wasn't supposed to tell you, but it seems like

you'd figure it out as soon as you woke up."

"Figure it out?" I repeat.

His eyes flick to my head, a reflex he's too slow to control, and I pull my hand from his grasp.

Gauze covers the side of my head. I trail my fingers around my hairline and find nothing but more gauze. I flatten my palm on the top of my skull. More gauze. And a tube. The monitor starts beeping again, but this time a nurse comes rushing through the door.

She gives Cameron a stern look as she pushes buttons to stop the beeping. "You should have told me she's awake."

He drops his hands. "It's only been a couple minutes."

"Go get her parents."

He gives my hand one last squeeze before leaving the room.

"What happened to me?"

She pauses with one hand over a plastic bag. "It's best we wait for the doctor. He can tell you exactly what they found."

"What they found?"

She smiles, a pitying expression that does nothing for her features. "Just be patient."

If there's anything I know, it's patience.

She leaves a few moments later. As soon as the door closes I swing my legs over the side of the bed and try to sit up, but the tangle of wires and tubes keep me in place. They also set off a new chorus of beeps and a particularly frightening alarm.

A stream of doctors and nurses crowd the room, followed by Mom and Dad, who stop in the doorway. I'm poked and jostled, but I don't feel any needles so I bite my tongue and wait for them to finish. Soon the beeping returns to normal and they file from the room.

All but one man, who I realize I know. Even without the EMT uniform.

"Martinez?"

He settles into the chair Cameron had been in minutes earlier. "Hi, Biz. I bet you didn't expect to see me here."

I glance at Mom and Dad, who are still hovering much too far away. "Do they have to wait over there?"

"No, of course not." He waves them closer and they press against the opposite side of the bed. Mom clutches my bandaged hand while Dad rests a shaky hand on my shoulder. "Your father found you collapsed in your home on Saturday and brought you here. Because of your history of headaches we did a CT-scan and found an abnormally large mass in your temporal lobe. My team agreed the mass was potentially life-threatening and had to be removed.

"The operation went smoothly. We won't have biopsy result for several more days, but so far your vitals have steadily improved and you should be released in about a week."

I touch Dad's fingers but continue to look at the doctor. "What does this mean for me?"

He straightens. "We're hopeful it means the end of your headaches. We'll continue to monitor you for quite some time, but I'm optimistic this will be the last time we'll see you in here."

Something still isn't making sense. "I thought you were an EMT."

He smiles. "Not exactly. I ride with the EMTs from time to time. It was part of our training in med school and I like the change of scenery." He shrugs, completely unapologetic for his deception. "I suspected something was wrong with you but thought if you knew I was a real doctor, you wouldn't listen to me."

"That's true." He still seems too young to be a brain doctor. "So you... fixed me?" A lump forms in my throat and I fight back tears. Right when I was beginning to accept that what I'd always thought of as a condition was something more, something that could actually help other people, it's gone.

After Dr. Martinez leaves, Mom goes on a coffee run, passing Cameron in the doorway. I haven't fully wrapped my mind around the idea that I can't flicker, but they seem to have something else on their minds.

Dad leans close and squeezes my hand. "Biz, honey, you did it."

I look back and forth between them. Cameron smiles down at me, and I'm taken aback by the change in him. A light shines from within him. "You look so… happy."

"That's because I am. Biz, they caught him. Because of you."

My head whips to Dad.

"I filled him in while you were unconscious. I wasn't sure if you told him a second time, but since you trusted him enough to tell him once, I thought you'd be okay with me telling him again."

I nod.

Cameron continues. "The police staked out the park and caught him trying to take a little girl." He shakes his head, a dazed look on his face. "I still can't believe it was Turner."

I touch the cut on my face. "Yeah, I know."

Dad covers my hand with his. "The police said that he

snapped when Jessica disappeared. They think he took the girls in some warped attempt to fix whatever he screwed up with his daughter."

Something still feels off. "So who's the guy I kept seeing?"

"He really was someone's dad, but not the way we thought." Cameron says. "His daughter disappeared a few years ago and when he heard about the kidnappings, he came here to... I don't know..."

"He said he hoped there was a connection to his daughter," Dad explains.

That explains the horrible expression on his face. "Do the police know what happened to the other girls?"

They exchange a look and Cameron sinks into a chair next to the bed. He clasps my hand, a broad smile lighting his face. "They found Katie."

My gaze whips between them. "Alive?"

They nod.

"But how? Where has she been?" When I set out to stop the kidnapper I thought if we were lucky, we'd find out what happened to Katie. I never in a million years imagined they'd find her alive.

Dad clears his throat. "Turner and his wife kept them in a

cabin out in the woods a couple hours from here. They found three other girls with Katie."

"What did he—" I stop. I shouldn't ask that. Not yet. "Is she... okay?"

He rests his forehead on the bed. "It's too soon to tell. Physically she seems healthy, but the doctors..." he trails off.

Dad touches my other hand. "She has a long recovery ahead of her."

The ache in my chest slowly shifts. It doesn't go away completely, but my breath comes a little easier. I squeeze Cameron's hand. "So she's really home?"

He looks up. Tears shine in his eyes. "All because of you."

I want to be happy. My plan worked. And any doubt about Cameron's involvement with Katie's disappearance are over. But I still have so many questions. Most importantly. "Does everyone know what I did?"

Dad touches the side of my face. "Nobody knows but us."

Chapter 39

ONE MONTH LATER

I'm standing in front of school, waiting for Mom to pick me up for an appointment with Dr. Martinez. Getting back into my routine hasn't been as difficult as I expected. Sure, it sucks that my long hair is gone, but not having headaches more than makes up for the unexpected 'do. Stride Right insisted I get tutors for Trig and English so I wouldn't fall any further behind, and as much as I can't stand him, it's kind of bizarre to have him looking out for me.

I'm still not driving, but between Cameron and Amelia I've been getting around okay. Dr. Martinez doesn't want me doing much, so I'm spending more and more time taking photos. The shot of Turner—the one that led to all this—never saw the light of day because I never returned to the park to take it. That was the day the police staked him out and my head nearly exploded.

I haven't been by the Strand yet. Or any other place where I've flickered. What's the point?

Although that's a little hard to do when I have to be ferried around by Mom, who's pulling up now.

"Sorry I'm late," she says as I climb into the car. "I had to juggle my lunch hour with one of the other women and she was late coming back."

"It's okay, Mom. We have plenty of time." I lean my head against the seat and close my eyes to the outside world. The trees make me the saddest. Even when it's cloudy, they remind me of everything that's been taken away from me.

The radio comes on and Mom's golden oldies fill the car. I open my eyes for the sole purpose to roll them, and am startled by the flickering light. I look around. We're in the Strand. Mom doesn't know anything about my ability so to her the Strand is just another stretch of road. I've never told her to avoid it.

The contrast between light and dark grows stronger, faster, and I close my eyes. A tear leaks out the corner. I lift my hand to wipe it before Mom sees, but freeze with my hand in front of my face.

I open my eyes.

Squeeze my fingers together.

And they start to tingle.

Coming Soon

FRACTURE

Melanie Hooyenga

Going back in time can't always save the future.

Acknowledgments

(also knows as my giant list of thank yous)

First and foremost, I'd like to thank my grandmother, Marian Walker, to whom this book is dedicated. The idea of FLICKER came to me while caring for her in the hospital, and a year later she read a draft, even though she's hardly my target audience.

Special thanks to: Stacey Graham, the best cheerleader and weird-hat-wearing friend a girl could ask for (will you please adopt me and add me to your brood?); Jason Tudor, my partner-in-tattoo and quieter cheerleader; Kristine McCombs, for sitting by my side while I finished the first draft; Scott Browne, my unintentional word-war partner who kept me going during NaNo; Natasha Fondren, the ebook formatting wizard who baby-stepped me through the technical side of things; and Erica Orloff, for freaking out when I shared my pitch and giving me the idea that this might be a story worth telling.

Thank you to my beta-readers: Nadine Semerau, my first—and most enthusiastic—reader, who never lost faith in me and withheld inspirational poems until I really, really needed one;

Valerie Kramin, without you Katie's story would have ended much differently; June "Bug" Kramin, your persistence has paid off; Rowyn Graham, your excitement in the story kept me going; Terri Lynn Coop, your brutal honesty made FLICKER the best it could be; and Erica Chapman, the absolute best writing friend ANYONE could have. Your plotting madness and determination that I make the one character who I had a soft spot for evil locked it all into place.

To my parents, Gary and Judy Hooyenga, for supporting me no matter what and reading a young adult novel more times than you probably care to.

For Jeremy, who wasn't in my life when I wrote FLICKER, but asked to read it very early in our relationship and has kept me going ever since.

Finally, to my Sisterhood of Snark. I would have cracked a long time ago without you by my side.

About the Author

Melanie Hooyenga has lived in Washington DC, Chicago, and Mexico, but has finally settled down in her home state of Michigan with her soon-to-be husband Jeremy. When not at her day job as a graphic designer, you can find Melanie attempting to wrangle her Miniature Schnauzer Owen and kicking Jeremy's butt at Kinect boxing.

Made in the USA
San Bernardino, CA
09 August 2014